I Am Good Enough for Me

Secrets to Self-Healing of not Good Enough:

Building a Bridge to Self-Acceptance, Self-Approval, and Self-Knowledge

Chipo Shambare, RN, Certified Midwife (retired) RMT, CSL, Ordained Minister, Keynote Speaker & Wholistic Coach

Copyright © 2009 Chipo Shambare.
All rights reserved.

ISBN: 1439271275
ISBN-13: 9781439271278
LCCN: 2010904506
CreateSpace Independent Publishing Platform
North Charleston, South Carolina

No portion of this book may be reproduced mechanically, electronically, or by any other means, including photocopying, without written permission of the publisher. It is illegal to copy this book, post it to a Web site, or distribute it by any other means without permission from the publisher.

Chipo Shambare

E-mail Address info@chiposhambare.com

Web site Address (www.healingbridge.ca)

Blog www.chipochemoyo.com

The author and publisher shall not be liable for your misuse of this material. This book is intended strictly for informational and educational purposes.

The purpose of this book is to educate and entertain. The author and/or publisher do not guarantee that anyone following these techniques, suggestions, tips, ideas, or strategies will become successful. The author and/or publisher shall have neither liability nor responsibility to anyone with respect to any loss or damage caused or alleged to be caused directly or indirectly by the information contained in this book.

Names used in the stories in this book have been changed to protect the identity of the people.

As the saying goes, "Love will build bridges." Let this healing bridge help you build 'Love Bridges' between you, your past and your present, as well as between you, your present, and your future, and between your outer and inner worlds.

There are things I find stop or block me from getting what I want, when I am stuck in my past or I am lamenting my future which I may never see happen.

The past is gone. Don't try to relive it.

I sometimes forget the present, which is the moment in which to be present—to be here and now - where life is happening. I encourage you to stay present and do your own exploration by writing and answering the questions in the book, any insights and use all the white spaces I left for you to write in.

Attend one of my workshops or presentations, and you will learn more about how to mine and uncover the diamond or gold that lies dormant deep within you.

I invite you to visit me at www.healingbridge.ca. Join my mailing list by completing the contact me form. Join my fan page on Facebook.

Acknowledgments

I would like to express my deeply felt gratitude to the Almighty God, my Creator, for being my guiding light and my rock.
To my mother and father in spirit, who believed in me, and who knew that I would make it in life and that I was good enough for me and the world.

To all my ancestors, who paved the way for me.

To all my teachers on earth and in the spirit world, for their guidance, encouragement, and support. To Caroline Myss who encouraged me to be healer God created.

I am especially thankful to my grandmothers, but most of all for my paternal grandmother, who passed down to me the gift of healing and who trusted in my aspirations.

Also to my dearest late Uncle Sketchly who taught me to love myself because I am good enough and trust strangers because a stranger is a friend you have not yet met or gotten to know, and can take into your heart and home.

To all the people who have trusted me and come to me in faith, seeking help in their healing journey.

To Lois and Paula, my dear friends, for being the first to help me get this book ready for editing.

My heartfelt gratitude to Mary Jennifer Brauner for the last minute tidying up of the book editing

Last but not least, my daughter, Melinda, for being who you are and for teaching me how to love and accept unconditionally.

About Me

Are you looking for the Author Chipo? Come over here. She is standing with courage on a bridge of integrated healing congruency, and honesty. Yes, this is me. I massage people's souls and teach them how to give birth to their true spirit as they heal their body, emotions, mind, and soul. I support them in letting go of the baggage "and unfinished business" that hold them back from becoming who they really are, a great person.

My background is in nursing, midwifery, natural medicine, such as nutrition consulting, massage therapy, and energy medicine. I am a professionally certified intuitive counselor and consultant, motivational public speaker, facilitator, trainer, and coach—and it all started in Zimbabwe, with my Shamanic paternal grandmother.

My life began as a student of the ancient Shamanic arts with her. I then learned Western teachings and returned, through hands-on therapies, to an all-encompassing, whole-body practice. I focus on helping people experience consciously what is going on within. As a clinically trained, multidisciplinary practitioner, I work with knowledge and intuition to help people heal their many defeated or shattered parts in order to become authentic and whole again.

With immense respect for the spiritual aspects that define us, I listen compassionately, without judgment or criticism, to the people in front of me or on the phone, to their physical and energetic bodies, **words, and welcome the true nature of their spirit and their many** "invisible" helpers who seek to guide their steps along their chosen path. I help them rediscover their healing bridge to their authentic, congruent self and feel good enough about who they are at that moment. It is my privilege, honor, and blessing to be the guide and the catalyst for healing.

Having come full circle before becoming a speaker spiritual counselor, I operated a very successful healing and teaching practice in Ottawa, Canada. In this practice, I combined traditional and complementary modalities, including the recognition of energies of the chakras, archetypal patterns, and healing through forgiveness.

Ottawa is home for now. I am a citizen of Planet Earth. I am an author of many articles. Mark Twain and other change teachers and writers have said something like (paraphrased) "Life is about stepping outside our comfort zones to meet and master change. The journey is sometimes a struggle, and for this we should be glad. If the struggle were taken away, we would feel no triumph when we succeed. Resisting the struggle and avoiding change and transformation is a losing battle, because these are the things that keep us truly alive."

I do not advocate passive surrender to anything because that is no kind of life to live. I am your catalyst agent, empowering you to engage joyfully in the challenge that change brings and empowering your transformation.

I teach and guide you on how to release the blocks or baggage you carry; to take ownership of your struggle whatever that may look like; and to celebrate the peace you find when the transformation is complete and the battle is won. I teach you how to return home where you began—not your physical home but your inner home. I help you remember the moment you decided to begin your profession, your business, or the relationship you may now find a struggle.

My unique personal interactive workshops and one-on-one sessions are designed to enable, enhance, and inspire self-growth and change. My clients experience extraordinary outcomes. I call myself "an agent for inner conflict change and management."

Testimonials

"Sue LeShien is a Certified Natural Health Practitioner (CNHP), Certified Holistic Aromatherapist Registered Reflexology Practitioner (RRPr), Usui/Tibetan Reiki Master in Ottawa Canada. Sue met Chipo when she was looking for reflexology practicum clients while she was studying for her reflexology certification. She not only found a client to practice on, she found a mentor and coach."

- ♥ Chipo's gentle spirit and strong, sure guidance helped me reach new depths of awareness.
- ♥ If you plan to attend just one retreat this year, make sure Chipo Shambare is a presenter!
- ♥ You won't recognize yourself after a session with Chipo! She's incredible!

Foreword

This is not your ordinary self-help or personal development book.

Book stores and the internet are filled with many books and eBooks on this subject. Most of these books claim to help you become a better person, but the content is from a textbook approach or point of view. They are written intellectually. This book, however, is written from the heart and asks you challenging questions that if you answer honestly, can change your life.

I am Good Enough for Me is profound because, when we don't feel good enough about ourselves that self poison drips down into all areas of our lives such as our work, our goals, and our ability to achieve our goals. It even affects the love we receive or not receive from others. In the end all areas of our life (spiritual, relationships, and work) suffers if we stay in this negative foggy place.

This book is about self-care and will help you to see what lowers your confidence in the world around you.

I am Good Enough For Me will help you look at your life, where you have been, where you are now and where you are going. Most of all, it examines your inner life with its conflicts, what stops you from moving forward and gives you the power to face the blocks, change and live an authentic life.

As the saying goes, "nobody is perfect". Too often people tend to obsess about what they don't like about themselves.

People who do this don't give themselves and others a chance to notice all the things about them that are great.

Almost everyone feels insecure sometimes, but self-confident people don't let those doubts control them and that is what makes them self-empowered.

You walk into the world differently when you "know" that you are good enough.

The real truth is… you are a brilliant light, meant for a purpose. When you understand this, not only is your head up high, but you enter the world with calm power. You no longer need to prove your worth to others or even to yourself. You just know, and that is enough.

That is pure personal power.

You will no longer be swayed off balance by others thoughts or actions, and no longer are you chasing empty dreams that you believe will make you more worthy.

You simply ARE. You simply BE.

Congratulations for taking this step into your own self-empowerment.

Enjoy the journey,
Stefanie Hartman

Speaker, Author, The New Income Architect
www.StefanieHartman.com

Table of Contents

Chapter 1
Feeling Not Enough While Growing
Up Is My Healing Medicine . . . . pg. 1

Chapter 2
Stress and Feeling Overwhelmed . . . . pg. 27

Chapter 3
Culture and Ancestory . . . . pg. 35

Chapter 4
Your Life Story . . . . pg. 41

Chapter 5
Invisible Support and Guides . . . . pg. 47

Chapter 6
Emotions . . . . pg. 53

Chapter 7
The Human Body . . . . pg. 59

Chapter 8
Spirit and Soul . . . . pg. 67

Chapter 9
Intuition and Self-Esteem . . . . pg. 77

Chapter 10
Forgiveness and Compassion . . . . pg. 85

Chapter 11
Prayer and Meditation . . . . pg. 89

Introduction

The principles of change, self-healing, and transformation are available to each and every person who is ready to let go of his or her hidden blocks, UNresolved issues, and UNfinished business. Perhaps you may have read many self-help books, attended many workshops and seminars, and feel that you have done all this self-exploration.

Why should you read another self-development book?

Good question. We are made of many layers that keep unraveling like the layers of an onion.

Research time: take an onion, cut it in half, and put it in a plastic bag or not; then leave it in the fridge and observe what happens. New layers will start to grow inside as old layers dry up.

There are many entrances to a mansion or house such as the front, back, and side doors; windows, and, for someone like Santa, the chimney. With this text, I am giving you another opening to enter your being or a new set of lenses or glasses to see through—another perspective.

If you are willing to be open and rediscover another layer of your being that needs to heal. Allowing you to be more of who you are here to be, and if you are willing to listen with your inner ear, learn a different language and hear the true nature of your soul, then you have found the right book.

Some of us were given or not given the positive guidance or encouragement to allow the expression of the true nature of our spirit to bloom; we grew up with mixed messages that retarded our spiritual growth. In most cases like this, we suppress, alter, limit, and deny our real nature and create the person we think and believe we are "supposed" to be.

Michelangelo once said, *"Every block of stone has a statue inside it, and it is the task of the sculptor to discover it."* I am hoping to help you see the statue inside of you, or as I say "mine the diamond or the gold within."

Here is another one of Michelangelo's quotes: *"I saw the angel in the marble and carved until I set him free."* Can you set the angel within free?

As I was writing this book, I remembered these quotes that I had read when I began my own healing work. They sure spoke of the work on which I was embarking, which helped me to see that the jewel or angel was within, but I had blocked it with my fears, unfinished or unresolved business, such as judgments, assumptions, and many other emotions and beliefs about who I was.

Seek and you will find; knock and the door will open. Are you ready for the ride? Here are a couple questions to ask yourself and answer honestly:

What are you looking for in your life on earth?

What are you willing to give up in order to find the true you that you love, trust, and believe in –to find the 'you' that says, "You are enough already."

Is it the you that you have given up for the people you love, the people who introduced you to the not-good-enough syndrome?

For this, I suggest you use the space provided or your journal to answer this question. Take some time to do this. I will be waiting for you.

Remember to be honest with yourself for your own healing; it is said honesty is the best medicine.

Introduction

This book is written to help those who are ready and willing to hear and find the truth about who they are and the truth about what holds them back from being their true self.

Its purpose is to help you stop living with inner conflict, torture, or torment. I had lived all my life with inner conflict, and the unfinished business the self-inflicted suffering was affecting my personal and professional life. After going through much physical pain and frequent emotional turmoil, with the medical model not able to find what was wrong with me, I decided to follow a different route. I began my inner work to do something about my unspoken pain, my unforgiving heart, my broken spirit, and self-inflicted suffering. I chose to make me a better person for me and not for others because that will happen naturally. I decided to change how I felt about myself, my life, those close to me, and the world. I wanted to please those around me at the expense of my own inner feelings and guidance; I decided to take personal responsibility and not blame things outside of me. I discovered that I was attracting things, situations, life, and people I did not necessarily want into my life. Healing myself meant I had to wake up, see what was going on inside and around me, and be aware of the meaning of what I was attracting into my life.

My intention is to help you explore what is going on within and become aware of whatever gets triggered mentally, emotionally, and physically. My goal is to help you become conscious of how you react or respond to outside stimuli.

As you read this book, if any part of you is touched or something is triggered by my way of writing or speaking, ask yourself, "Why am I feeling or thinking this way?" Maybe there is a little bit of some old "not good enough" feeling or a buried emotional something ready to be set free. Only your truth shall set you free.

This book is an inward journey to help you heal yourself.

It is to help you be the best you can be regardless of what anyone says or has said in the past. Are you the person you were meant to be? Or the person you feel you can be?

You know you can be more, and I believe in you 100 percent. All you have to do is do the work that is necessary. The information in this book comes with the theory that you are good enough, you are enough, and that everything you need to be your best is within you. You have all the answers for you: all you need to do is stop, become aware, listen—listen with your heart—and take action. You know what I am talking about. You have done it and heard it before, and, yes, you can do it. You have the power to hear your spirit speak and give you guidance. The more you practice, the easier it will become. You will get there. I am sure you've heard this story before. Here is Rabbi Arthur Waskow's version.

"A visitor, poring with a puzzled face over an arcane map, stops a New Yorker on the street and asks, 'How do you get to Carnegie Hall?' Says the world-weary New Yorker, 'Practice, practice, practice!'"

So, if you want to get to your "inner Carnegie Hall," practice, practice. This book will remind you of who you really are. It will challenge you to move from your comfort zone to what Gail Larsen of *Real Speaking* calls the "home zone." This is the place of truth, maybe a place where you feel vulnerable but connected and grounded; you feel solid in your truth when you are in that place that Larsen calls the home zone, and the connection you have with the zone is felt very deeply within. Most people shy away from this place as it is considered emotional. I am sure you have heard the expression "I am in the zone." If you are honest with yourself, you'll admit that things can get emotional at your physical home. Is it not that we keep our family secrets locked at home, in our private inner home, our hearts?

Introduction

In this book you will be reminded to do simple things you already know if you choose to take the plunge. You will be reminded that where there is a will, there is a way. As long as you have the desire, belief, and expectancy, you can do it with a little help from your friends, physical and nonphysical.

This information will help you open doors that you or someone else shut or blocked a long time ago. It's okay—you will not find any monsters you cannot conquer or slay. They are ready to leave as they don't want to stay in the dark anymore. Remember you will recall what you choose to remember when you are ready. You are never given what you are not ready for, so relax my friend, it's all good.

Best of all, your body talks to you all the time and it will continue to do so as you explore. Your body remembers everything that ever happened to you. It has the memory of an elephant. It remembers everything from pre birth to now, and whatever is locked in, sure doesn't want to be shut in anymore. When you are sick, it's the body's way of communicating with you. "Just listen up. Your body is talking." I am not advocating doing away with your health care providers. I am saying help them—work as a team and get involved in your health and healing. If everyone does his or her part, I am sure every nation's health system would be healthier than it is now. Let's get to work to heal the self as you help to unload and heal your national health care system. Be the proactive person you can be and trust yourself. Mahatma Gandhi said, "You must be the change you want to see in the world."

Inspirational Quote

"Ver dese Vie deise Vay," Where there is a will there is a way, quoting Mother Superior at my boarding school.

On Hope:

"Once I knew only darkness and stillness. My life was without past or future. But a little word from the fingers of another fell into my hand that clutched at emptiness and my heart leaped to the rapture of living."

Helen Keller

Write your inspirational quote here.

Chapter 1

FEELING NOT ENOUGH WHILE GROWING UP IS MY HEALING MEDICINE

"Sometimes I think [my husband] is so amazing that I don't know why he's with me. I don't know whether I'm good enough. But if I make him happy, then I'm everything I want to be" Angelina Jolie American actress, b. 1975 from http://www.brainyquote.com/quotes/quotes/a/angelinajo128014.html

This quote attracted me because she is talking about the subject of being good enough for other people. Many people often think or feel like Angelina. Are we here to make others happy? Make them happy and us unhappy? If a person grew up thinking and believing that making other people happy is the most important thing. What kind of life would that person have?

I call this kind of belief "people pleasers." What are your thoughts? How much or how often did you please others, including parents, siblings, teachers, elders, and the list goes on. Take inventory of your people pleasing pattern or not. Be honest with yourself. I believe that honesty is the best healing policy.

How good enough is related to self-development and self-esteem, and can heal your not good enoughness (a word I made up).

Discovering how good enough you were as a child and YOU as an adult. Can you hear the song in this? I can hear it because I have sung this song too long.

Yes, you can because it's time for you to start singing a different song and singing your own praises in a song, to shout out I am good enough for me. It doesn't matter even if someone told you that you can't sing. Remember this quote from Marianne Williamson, "Our deepest fear is not that we are inadequate. Our deepest fear is that we are powerful beyond measure. It is our light, not our darkness that most frightens us. We ask ourselves, who am I to be brilliant, gorgeous, talented, and fabulous? Actually, who are you not to be? You are a child of God. Your playing small does not serve the world. There is nothing enlightened about shrinking so that other people won't feel insecure around you. We are all meant to shine, as children do. We were born to make manifest the glory of God that is within us. It's not just in some of us; it's in everyone. And as we let our own light shine, we unconsciously give other people permission to do the same. As we are liberated from our own fear, our presence automatically liberates others." Therefore who are you, and who am I, to feel you and I are "Not Good Enough"? When we were little kids, somehow something was misunderstood, and we retained the wrong message from those who raised us that we are inadequate. We do misunderstand each other, including ourselves and what we think we heard and understood. During a communication class in massage school, I wrote, "I thought you understood what I thought I said and what I meant to say, but you didn't understand what I thought I said and I meant to say." Communication becomes very convoluted for the human mind to understand. In the communication process, we take in information in many ways—intellectually through words, physically through our body, visually through our eyes. Our energy field takes it all in. Whatever is being communicated to us or what is happening around us is taken in by our whole being.

As you were growing up, were you ever told that you were not good enough? Were there situations where you felt that you were not good enough? I hear many different versions of this kind of put-down.

I was told and heard this kind of unworthiness during my younger years. Despite all odds, I survived all the put-downs, unworthiness, and the feelings of being not good enough. I now hold a degree in G.E. (Good Enough) from the University of Good Enough Self-Development and Healing.

Over my twenty years of exploring self-healing for myself and facilitating as a healer with hundreds of people seeking healing for the physical body, mind, emotions, or relationships, I have discovered that the majority of people had deep struggles or conflicting feelings about not feeling good enoughitis (a new word I made up). They could be very successful in their professional and personal lives, but they carried some stuffed emotions like pain, anger, guilt, resentment, shame, and depression from their childhood. They felt that something was not feeling right or that there was an internal war going on. Remember how impressionable you were as a child. Remember how you looked up to an adult and imitated that person and maybe said to yourself, "I want to be like auntie or uncle so and so when I grow up." I did that, and when I grew up, yes, I was like my admired adults, with all their good, bad, and not-so-good characteristics, feelings, and behaviors.

In my growing up years, I did not realize how vulnerable I was to what was happening in my life and around me. I didn't realize that I was a creative sponge. Most of all I didn't know that perhaps my upbringing may have left some wounds, unresolved or unfinished business, and blocks that may have prevented me from seeing how good I was. It wasn't until I was sick and tired of being sick and tired that I decided to investigate and do something about the unpleasant life I was living. Could it be true for you that your adult self might be affected by what the younger you learned, experienced, felt, saw, were told, or heard? Could you have tucked it in somewhere deep within you?

Try to write your timeline through the eyes and feelings of the younger you, to see what you remember or recall. Also, see if some emotions or feelings come up. You may choose to write about one situation and see where the feelings are located in your body or mind and what words come up. Explore and see where this takes you. This is all about paying attention, taking action to resolve the inner conflict, making choices, and not taking anything personally. Listen to the stories you tell yourself and others about your upbringing. Ask your parents or whoever raised you (if they are still alive), about you, your family, and what you were like as a child What comes for you while listening to the stories is important, listen for the feelings.

As a storyteller, I love to speak and tell stories. I invite you to delve into your own stories and see if there are any charges or blocks. The charged stories are the healing ones. They let you know that you hit on something that doesn't belong there. At the beginning, it is not comfortable or easy. After a while you will thank yourself, as the emotionally charged and hidden issue that was causing inner discomfort or conflict is released or gone.

Caution! Travel into the world of your unknown with grace, love, honor, honesty, respect, and integrity. Take care not to project what you find there. People tend to go on the blame game and project onto someone else as if whatever they just mined or discovered was the other person's fault. This could be an emotion like shame, anger, pain, joy, great peace, or something you had forgotten. Remember not to point your blame finger at whatever target was or is closest to you.

Feeling Not Enough While Growing Up Is My Healing Medicine

Let me tell a story I heard a long time ago, I am paraphrasing it here. Imagine a set of twin girls raised in a dysfunctional family with an abusive father who would beat them up and tell them all kinds of negative things about themselves. One left home at the age of seventeen and went to live on her own. The other stayed at home.

Now! Imagine interviewing these girls when they are over twenty-five years old. Maybe the one who left home went to college and is now successful and has a very well-paying professional job. When asked why she is different from her twin sister, she says, "I realized at a very young age that I didn't want to live with abuse and feeling like I am some trash. I made up my mind to get out of there. I always got into trouble with my dad because I stood up to him. I learned that I am a somebody, and he was just making sure I was strong enough to be in the world."

When the other twin was asked why she wasn't as successful as her sister she said, "How can I be with my dad beating me up all the time and telling me that I will never amount to anything because I am not good enough for anything or anybody."

I heard stories like this when I had my full-time healing practice.

Millicent sent her fiancé Stan who was expressing unbeneficial behavior at home and work of which Millicent disapproved. She had given him an ultimatum that if he didn't do something about it, the relationship was over. Seeing these two together, you couldn't see the signs described by Millicent unless you had a trained eye or your intuitive sense was on high alert.

Remember, that those who raised us also programmed us for life for good and for not so good. The things they say or do to us and the way they raised us gets logged into our system, which means into our body, mind, emotions, and our biology. The stories we heard about everything are recorded into our being.

When I was growing up, some of the punishments used were the belt or stick. My dear nuns would use prayer. We had to go kneel down and pray for the prescribed time. Talk about a put off to prayer and God.

The gentleman did call for an appointment, and during the history taking, he did not mention the reason why he had come.

As we began the body massage session, I could feel how his body was like concrete. It was solid like a rock, but nothing to do with him being a heavyweight or someone who pumps iron. The body was holding all sorts of emotions. I asked him how his body felt, and he said, "I am in so much pain. You have no idea."

I like to gently push the envelope, so I asked what kind of pain it was, how long he'd had it, and when had it begun. As we talked the body was softening, and all of a sudden this burst of anger came out as he related to the issue his wife-to-be had mentioned. He entered into the power of the emotion as he related the story how his mother had made him so angry that he put a fist through the wall. I could feel the emotion in the room. If I had not been aware of how emotions work, I would been scared and run out of the room. The concrete I had felt in his body initially was now a lot softer.

Remember that the body is like a shock absorber, and it absorbs everything—the good, the bad, and the ugly. As he related the story with his mother, he said, "I can never be good enough for her, and I will never be or do anything good enough for her." I believe these words or something similar echoes in almost everyone. It doesn't matter how old or where you come from. As I probed about his childhood, he related the dysfunction he grew up with and how he had taken it all into his body tissues.

Visit your own time line to see if there is any not good enoughness in one form or another. Examine how your upbringing, family, authority, school, and friends were. What I have witnessed professionally over many years is that we humans hold on to everything and especially things that do not serve us at all. Most of what we hold is hidden from our consciousness. It's like a blind spot. Even when the person who did us wrong is no longer with us or is dead, we still feel the not good enough that they told us we were. It's almost like we are holding onto the pain they caused us in order to punish them. How profound is that?

Take some time to write what has come up for you. Writing is a way of expressing what is hidden. I believe you are never given what you cannot handle. If you find that you are given too much stop and process, and or seek help from a professional or a wise trusted friend even relative.

As children, we were raised by adults who have their own lessons, baggage, challenges, fears—their own mixture of emotions and unfinished business. They accumulated loads of stuff that sometimes they just let out, and they did their best with what they knew then. Maybe the way they raised you is the way they were raised. Now that you are an adult how do you view your childhood? How are you doing with your own gifts, fears, old memories, and the baggage you have brought with you around your own kids, friends, your significant other, siblings, coworkers, the boss, the world, authority, and yourself?

Are you good enough for you? I say YES to your good enoughness to you.

Let's go back in time and look at your upbringing. How was it? Do you have snapshots or a movie? Are they in black and white or color? What do they show, and who is in them? Do you hear voices? What are they saying? Whose voices are they? What do you think and feel when you look at your time line?

I invite you to pay attention to the body sensations, memories, thoughts, feelings, and even your own behavior that shows up when you are reading and trying to make sense of what you are reading and the writing you are asked to do.

I have realized that time does heal. The way I was growing up and who and how I am today are two different people. I am sure you are the same; if you don't feel that way, hang in there and have faith in who you really are because with continuing self development, it will happen. I did it and have pursued my dreams such as education and travel. I have become a very successful, professional businesswoman and healer, despite what I heard growing up and what I continued to tell myself like I would never amount to anything and I wasn't good enough. Despite all that I heard about how I was a nobody, I made it to tell the story. What happened? I had a dream, and that dream and I became a somebody. You can too you have already made it this far. Regardless of where or how you were raised, you have made it. Can you see where you have come from and where you are now? You turned things around, and if you think you haven't, you can turn your life around no matter what your age. You can do it! Try this mantra "I am good enough for me". Keep repeating it until you feel it inside of you—until you believe it.

Here is a snapshot of my story; keep yours in mind as you read on.

I was born and raised in Zimbabwe during the segregation era, when Africans and whites did not live happily together—or ever after! I was raised by missionaries, and by parents who worked for the missionaries and who at times thought they were missionaries because they tried to fit into the missionaries' mold. At least their jobs paid for our school fees.

Education was a big thing in those days in Zimbabwe, and it became my mission, my driving force—to be educated and leave the country. Our neighbor to the south, South Africa, was deeper into apartheid, but Zimbabwe had its fair share of segregation. I suffered a lot of put-downs, shame, and inferiority complexes. The most memories I have are of inner conflict; being unable to speak-up; stifling negative emotions such as anger, shame, and guilt; and wanting to live far away from my birth country. As a young, sensitive, creative child, I must have added more inner drama; while on the outside I was a very well-behaved and compliant child, at times when I was pushed enough I got so angry that I could feel the injustice boiling inside.

I am inviting you to transcribe your story; the way you remember it and take what comes up as being from your wise self. Please don't get tangled up in emotionality and don't overwhelmed by it all. Take a break because what you need now is to let your ego self, the intellect, tell its story. It needs to be heard; perhaps it has never been heard by anybody, especially by you, the owner. At the same time, the emotional body will want to be free; allow it to express itself.

Now it's time to be the parent and listen to your inner child!

In my upbringing, whether male or female, some of us were constantly reminded that we had too much skin pigmentation and could never expect to succeed at anything in life. We were never looked at as equals or bright or gorgeous or brilliant. My self-confidence and self-esteem were significantly below the radar. I did not want to be heard, listened to, or accepted. Who was I to think I should be visible? In my mind I was a nobody.

What about you? Were you listened to at all? How did you feel when the adults around you ignored you? Now listen to yourself—what do you hear and what are you saying? Maybe your adults were enlightened, and they praised and acknowledged you.

Despite all that went on in your life, you are here to tell the story.

Was your upbringing like mine? Mine was suppression and oppression. At the same time, there was something within me that was strong and powerful. It guided, encouraged, pushed, and gave me the power and strength to go on and make my dreams come true.

What about you and your inner genie deep within? Did you listen, take notes, and follow through? You, too, have a very powerful presence that is continuously guiding, nurturing, and accompanying you wherever you go. Childhood time is a very interesting time in which to be programmed, taught, molded, shaped, and prepared for upcoming adulthood.

I did more than was expected from the very beginning of my life. The feeling of something deep within leading and guiding the way, whatever this is, is present day and night, ready, willing, and able to be your invisible partner—and guess what. You don't have to pay for it. When you feel good enough you accept the help.

I call this *relentless inner power*. Mine helped me to know what I wanted, and it encouraged me to listen to and follow my heart's desire. I suppose at a subconscious level I felt good enough. I wanted to be educated, to be a somebody, and to travel. I told myself that I had to get out of what I believed to be a miserable life, thinking life was better on the other side of the apartheid wall.

We all have stories about our upbringing. These stories have shaped us. If it wasn't for these stories, you wouldn't be you and I wouldn't be me. What about you? How is your story shaping you? What were your circumstances when you were growing up? Did you, or shall I say, do you, listen to that something deep within that is helping you follow the map of your destiny? Do you say to yourself, "I knew that" or "I should have listened to my gut feelings or heart" or "I knew that wasn't right for me"? Even though the not good enough rhyme was being sung around you, you can be what your heart is directing you to be. Just listen and follow. Are you ready to change your story?

Take some time to answer the questions above.

A friend always says "everything that happens to us in our lives is there for a reason and that reason is there to save you." With all the things that may not have been so good as I was growing up, looking back with what I have learnt about myself, I am grateful that it all happened. Those things made me want to change and be a much better person. I chose not to live with all the many voices in my head and the feelings I was feeling.

What I heard inside my head, when I gave myself the time to listen, was conflict, many voices saying many different things. It felt like there was a battle or a war going on. I felt confused, mixed up, and numb, and I just went through the motions of acquiring education. Remember that, this was my mission. Looking back, I think I was very resistant to the education I was seeking, and I was also defiant of my educators. I couldn't verbalize what was going on inside, and I blamed the educators, my parents, society, the government, politics, religion—you name it, it was at fault. Do you ever do that? Do you point fingers at others and not examine yourself?

In my head I detected over and over that there was something wrong with me because I imagined that other people could see it. I accepted that they were right and I was wrong. At the same time I did everything possible to prove them wrong. My mantra was, "Watch me". I set goals for myself, and I reached them! I played the watch-me game with them and myself. What is your mantra and how do you encourage yourself to keep going regardless of what people say or what you think people are saying? Write down words of strength or words of encouragement you normally say to yourself or to others when you are down. Make that your mantra.

My deepest wish was to see the world and explore, even though whenever I mentioned my dream, I was reminded that no Africans ever did that. What was your deepest wish as a child? Has it come to pass? Perhaps you are still too young. If you are young, dream and dream big! Don't let anything get in the way. Reading books like this is the greatest gift you can give yourself as a young person because it tells me you are open for transformation. When I was in grade 3 the teacher asked the students what each wanted to do when they grew up. I raised my hand high and said, "I am going to live in Canada." The whole class, including the teacher, laughed. She said, "How are you going to do that? You are an African living in Zimbabwe with no money." I said, "I will go by plane."

That dream and many others did come true! I went to Oxford, England, to finish my studies. Remembering what I had heard about England and what I saw, I was disappointed

I Am Good Enough For Me

about my discovery. My memory of that experience was different than what I expected and what I found was a hugely different way of life, especially the way people treated one another. The way children were raised was in a way similar to mine even though the houses, the beliefs, and the values were different.

I did find that even the people in England felt not good enough about themselves. As I started to wonder if I had made a mistake, I started to think about Wilson Pickett's song, "Don't let green grass fool you; the grass may be greener on the other side." Well, guess what? My not good enough rhyme followed me to England and to Canada. Where have you found similarities and differences in the way you were raised? It was not much different from my birth country! I noticed that people were treated and felt the same way as I did growing up, even though the segregation was not the same. I still heard the same famous words not good enough. I could feel that their attitudes were the same as those of people in my home village, and they felt the same way as I did. I realized we are all the same, and we act, react, and behave the same. Even though we may be raised in different countries by different people, we are still very similar.

Even having had all the successes I have listed, I still felt not good enough in my new hometown. Yet people did have more privileges and opportunities than I had in Zimbabwe, where I wished all Africans could have what North Americans have. What about you? What have you discovered in your travels about others, beliefs, values, aspirations, opportunities, and the way children are raised?

I am hoping you are getting some insight about your own life's journey and into what is blocking or stopping your transformation and keeping you from living your life's dream. In order for our dreams to manifest, we sometimes must face our shadows, our negative side and feelings. We are creatures of many facets. Become aware of all you are, accept all parts of you, work with them, and transform them into the integrated you that you want to be. You don't have to act out the shadow self—it's only reminding you that it's there, pay attention.

I began my quest to find out why I felt this certain way, why I felt that people were thinking or saying, "Chipo, you are not good enough!" No one actually told me that to my face. I had internalized all the old stories from my childhood, and I just imagined that people thought I am not good enough. Besides all my thinking about not being good enough, I also felt it in my gut. Ouch that hurts.

I actually had an ulcer in my (duodenum) gut, which I now realize came from the internal conflict and undigested emotions and feelings, and not necessarily the physical foods I was eating.

As a young child and then woman, I had pushed those feelings deep down into my subconscious. It was only much later in my life that I began to explore them. Then I was feeling horrible and I was actually becoming physically ill. I didn't like myself. It was only when I began to explore the concept of self-development and self-healing that I realized the answers to my feelings of unworthiness were buried within me.

One of the feelings/questions that have been stuck in the deep back pocket of my psyche was and is: why was I born with so much pigmentation in my skin? Why was I born in Africa and negatively perceived as if I am wrong, bad, and not good enough? This is the toughest issue for me, an issue I haven't yet resolved. To be totally healed of the darkness that I carry, day in and day out, will be very interesting. It will be interesting to see what I would become. I believe I will become more accepting of myself as I transform my feelings and as I continue this self- development journey. Is there an aspect of you that you struggle to accept or reconcile?

It's about opening and closing doors. Be an optimist.

"When one door of happiness closes, another opens; but often we look so long at the closed door that we do not see the one which has been opened for us." Helen Keller

You may ask yourself, "What did Chipo do and is she all healed?" There are some parts I feel are healed, but I am still exploring many other parts. No, I am not all healed, and I don't think I will be all healed. The purpose of this book is to help you, by sharing my experiences, if you are ready and willing to explore your psychophysiology.

As a child at boarding school, I lived in isolation for about three to four months because the nuns said I possibly had rheumatic fever or polio and an ulcer in my duodenum. Were all these body responses due to too many emotions or unresolved issues that I held inside me? Dr. Caroline Myss, author of Anatomy of the Spirit, says, "Your biography becomes your biology." This concept makes a lot of sense to me. Check it out.

Now, ask yourself some of the key questions that I have asked myself many times. How do you feel about yourself? Are you good enough for you? Will you ever be good enough? Have you ever been good enough? What do you want to do about it? What can you do about it?

What is your standard of yourself? Did you grow up hearing these or similar words? "Not good enough." "You will never amount to anything." "You are useless." "You are stupid." I am sure you could make up your own list or versions of not good enough!

Continue on. Discover how "not good enough" can turn into "good enough" for you.

I hope you are allowing some of these thoughts and emotion-provoking questions to sink in and be answered by the deepest part of your being. I recommend you take some time to regroup and see where these questions are taking you.

I am going to talk about how the way we were raised negatively or positively affected and still affects our adult life. We can objectively examine our past without crucifying, blaming, judging, or victimizing others or ourselves for what happened.

I like this quote from Robert Munro, "Everyone is guilty, but no one is to blame." This means that responsible for doing something we are not proud of but we don't need to feel badly or worthless for what happened or the outcome.

Let's be objective about our examination. Make the self-assessment short. Take what you learned, what is working or not, and what can you do to change your life, and let the rest go. As children, we were very impressionable. We believed and accepted everything as truth and took everything personally. Everything shaped who we are today.

What I have discovered for myself is that all that happened to me affected my self-esteem, self-acceptance, self-approval, self-acknowledgement, and self-expression; now that I am developing myself, my self-esteem is getting better and stronger. I am becoming esteemed. I am sure most people reading this have similar memories of their upbringing.

If what you are finding in this book rings a bell, makes sense, helps you to see your own timeline, or you feel some connection to what you are reading then, I invite you to continue examining how you feel about yourself and others. Consider how you can start to do something to feel good about yourself, to move on, become who you want to become and get on with your life.

Now think about your life from beginning to now. Use the space provided or have a pad of paper and pen nearby to write. You can close your eyes if you wish. This will help to shut out outside distractions and let that part of you that knows everything about you take you on an inner journey. Allow yourself to be objective and detached from the outcome and to become the detective of your soul's journey.

You can take mental notes of what happened, what you saw, heard, and most of all, what you felt, and if you can, identify what you did with and about the feelings, who was involved, and what was the situation like. When you are finished, write down as much as you can remember. Don't worry about remembering everything. It's not what you remember, it's what you felt. If there is a purpose to recall, it will come with time. You will remember what you need to for now. Your memory will take you to situations that had a feeling memory because this was imprinted in your body and subconscious. Your body memory will bring out what you are ready to handle, and you are never given more than you can handle.

Feeling Not Enough While Growing Up Is My Healing Medicine

An example of my feeling not good enough would be when I was among my peers. I had feelings of failing in everything I would attempt, and feelings of not having money, which were all engrained deep into my psyche from way back when. Our parents, or those who raised us, did their best and were using all they knew and doing all they could to help shape us into what they thought was "good for us." Remember, we did not come with an operational manual like the appliances you buy from the store.

When and where, or in what circumstances, did you feel not good enough? Where in your life now would you say you feel not good enough?

As a child I never sat myself down to evaluate where I was going and where I was coming from. Unfortunately our parents did not do that either. If you could ask your parents and could do an examination of all areas of your family life, I think that would be a great family healing.

I think my father tried to do something similar to what I am saying, and I hated it and him for doing what we called "interrogation time." We would all be called to come into a circle, and he would ask how our day had been, and what we wanted to change and do about our lives. I can remember as I write this that it felt like being judged by him. I disliked it so much that sometime I would pretend to not be feeling well, and I would go to bed before the circle was called. He clued in very quickly and had me hauled out of bed.

Another way to self-examine would be to look at your life right now. Be brutally honest with yourself: where is it that your life is not working the way you want it to work? Don't hold back on yourself; this is a personal and private matter. I am not going to ask to read your writing—it's all yours. It is an inside job; no one is watching you. Go for it full on! Nobody needs to know you are working with some emotional or psychological stuff buried deep in the unconscious. Is there anything that you experienced in your past that is showing up now?

Using this self-examination process could be the beginning or continuation of your self-healing, and could lead to self-development, self-discovery, and bring out the true, the real you. Take a crack at it, see what you find and feel, and remember the truth about you. The truth shall set you free.

What do want out of your life? This life!

Do you know what your purpose is and are you aligned with it? If not, what is stopping you? What is blocking your journey to your heart's desire?

Since I was a little kid, my goal was to get an education, leave Africa, and travel. Yes my dreams came true. I became a

Feeling Not Enough While Growing Up Is My Healing Medicine

registered nurse, midwife, massage therapist and many other trainings. It was my dream to live in Canada, and I do. What was your dream at that young age? Do you remember it? Write it down. Did you achieve the dream or dreams? Time to write some more.

Do you think with all these accomplishments that I felt good enough about myself? Nooooooooo! Even though I left some of the people, the tribes that I believed were the cause of my feelings of not good enoughness, I realized that all those mixed or negative feelings and emotions from the messages I heard growing up were stuck somewhere deep inside me and would remain with me unless I chose to change them.

Let's come back to your life story now that you have done that short exercise of reevaluating your time line. List in hand and full of courage and determination, you say, "Okay, I am ready. I can't live this kind of life anymore. I want to change." Let's go back in time on an inner journey to face just one situation you discovered; pick a small one until you feel comfortable and confident with the process to tackle bigger issues.

Find a comfortable place to sit or to lie down, but no snoozing or going to sleep! Take three deep breaths in and out using your diaphragm and belly muscles.

With the inhalation, breathe in all the stress, feeling, and thoughts, and then let them out with every exhalation. After the three breaths or more if needed, go back in your imagination and visit the situation you found when you were told you were not good enough. Let the story relive itself. What is the situation about, who was there, what did you hear, see, say, and feel; where is the feeling in your body. There may be some changes that have taken place when you revisit that place or situation. You may feel different than you did when it happened, or you may feel the same.

Some people notice something has changed; others may take longer. Not to worry; sometimes we take baby steps. Don't expect giant steps at the beginning. I have found that the exercise works for me and for the people with whom I have worked. Be willing to examine your life and to stay open for what comes. Be open for options to look at the situation differently and don't be attached to the outcome or have any expectations of how it should play out.

Make sure when you do any self-healing that you have an intention in mind. Let it go and trust. Remember, energy follows thought and thoughts are energy. Forgive the other person or persons, or situation and most of all forgive you. Your intention is your thought. If I may caution you at this time not to sabotage yourself. As one of my teachers, Dr. Norm Shealy, says about sabotage, "Don't shoot yourself in the foot." I know the saboteur very well; it is that part that will say you are fine the way you are or give some lame excuse. This aspect is in all of us, and it works very well with the part that says poor me, look at what they did to me. This is the blaming part, the finger pointer, and what I call the victim. I am sure you know what I am talking about.

I still have some residue, some recorded messages that keep playing—messages from my mother, my sister Mary, my father, and all those adults who raised and helped shape my life. I also had an important role model, my auntie, whom I wanted to take after. She was sharp, with lots of attitude. My father adored me, but when I didn't live up to his expectations, the not good enough lecture came up. The victim in me likes to hold on to these messages.

Now it's your turn. You can choose to examine yourself. Ask yourself: What may still be holding me back? What are some of the residues that the broken record or stuck tape that keeps playing? Perhaps you have achieved every goal you set for yourself, and you say to yourself, "I have done all my work." Maybe you have no self put-downs. If so, I congratulate you, and I challenge you to ask yourself, "What else might still be there that's preventing me from _____?" Fill in the blank. Keep reaching higher and higher.

If you're like me, welcome, my friend, to my world—or to the human world of not good enough. We have work to do because the Creator doesn't create people who are not good enough.

Over time, when you decide that enough is enough already, when you cannot stand yourself, some parts of your life, your job, or whatever is missing or not going well for you, could it be it's because your self-esteem is so low that you cannot stand up for your soul? Are you aware when you are stressed or under pressure? How do you know that you are stressed? What do you do to relieve yourself of that pressure?

I encourage you to self-examine so that you can start to know the difference between when you are stressed and when you are not. Give yourself permission to face the situation or the person that you feel or think is stressing you and then be able to face the fear, the anger, and whatever else that may come up when you confront the cause of your stress. Take the plunge and do whatever it takes to conquer the fear. Our mind does a very good job of creating a mountain out of nothing. Pay attention it is freaking out most of the time,

Remember, our thoughts are like prayers. We are always praying, and our prayers are answered in some form or another through what materializes in our physical world.

I noticed the results I got came from what I was feeling, thinking, and seeing about myself and those around me. I attracted things and people similar to my thoughts. I decided to get help from different therapies in order to help me express my emotions and all the inner conflict. I went for body massage, mind, psychotherapy, and emotional therapy, spiritual therapy; I called it all physioemopyschospiritual (I made this word up) therapy. I mean look at the wholeness of your being.

I really wanted to dig deep into my being, and see and feel what was in my core, in my psychology, my emotional body, and my spiritual body. I wanted to see how deep I could go into all these areas to find out who I am. I invite you to do the same if you want to become authentically you and be congruent with your spirit.

Some principles of the human system I have discovered are that we are like a computer with its systems; we are designed to run on software that becomes outdated and needs to be upgraded. As the computer language goes, Garbage in, garbage out. When did you last upgrade or update your software? Maybe it's time. Start asking yourself, "Why am I not good enough?" questions. Or, "Why am I feeling whatever?" Fill in the blank. I think you're going to answer your own question. Do you have a virus scanner for your human system? Start to ask. What can I do to become good enough for me? How do I want to begin?

Write your answers down here.

Part of self-growth, awareness, development, and acceptance is to realize when you continue to reinforce beliefs about yourself or others into your own self-awareness; it becomes part of you and your self-image—positive, negative, or indifferent. Do yourself a favor. You owe it to yourself to be an adventurer and explorer of all of you.

Study you—don't just read books someone else has written. This is like a self-study course. It's all about you! Congratulations. You are on the right track.

Chapter 2

STRESS AND FEELING OVERWHELMED

Stress to me means pressure, overexertion, or putting too much weight on something.

Overwhelm means to be overcome by something, as with emotions, or when **perceptual stimuli sweep over, overpower, and overtake** such as in "I was drowning in work or overwhelmed with responsibility." "The noise drowned out her speech."

* Overpower: overcome by superior force something bigger than me.

When you are overwhelmed or overpowered and don't feel as good as someone else, you are in comparison mode, and you will run yourself down.

You think others are better than you; most of the time you and your mind are making it up and you get stressed. Most of the time we live in our heads creating stories about nothing real. The mind has a job to do, and the mind's job is protection. To protect you from what you don't yet know about you. I think the mind worries that if you change it may be out of a job. The mind wants you to believe that you are okay and safe where you are, so why change?

Here is a quote by Susan Jeffers, "Feel the Fear... And Do It Anyway"

"It is reported that more than 90 percent of what we worry about never happens. That means that our negative has less than a 10 percent chance of being correct. If this is so, isn't being positive more realistic than being negative? Think about your own life. I'll wager that most of what you worry about never happens."

This worry syndrome causes stress, and I believe that most of it comes from our feelings of inadequacy. Ladies, have you ever worried when going to a party or work about your outfit or your hair? If you are bold enough to ask a friend or coworker if they noticed anything amiss, most of the time they say they haven't unless they are good at lying. People are busy looking and worrying about themselves not about your outfit or hair. It's about them to them, and it's all about you to you; unfortunately we don't live our lives this way. It is always about what they may think or what they may say, whoever they are. We are so much looking for other people's approval instead of our own approval and acknowledgement.

I have discovered that all of this causes us stress and overwhelms us quickly and easily. Then we cannot function as well as we want to.

Here is a story about stress and overwhelming with Miss P. or Master P. (P stands for Perfect).

She/he had to get A's in school and studied long and hard to please Mum and Dad because that's what they expected from Miss/Master P., even though they didn't quite say it that way. They just wanted him/her to succeed and make a better life. They are successful, and they want this for their own offspring. In this environment, the intellectual is on top of the list, and the inner wisdom is forgotten and is not nurtured. Miss/Master P.'s creative aspect may not have been acknowledged and nurtured by the intellect.

The point here is that sometimes we follow someone else's wishes or dream such as following our parents' wishes and dreams instead of our own wishes and dreams. Perhaps we are not enjoying the career that was chosen for us and this can cause stress in our life.

Managing your daily stresses in a beneficial way and knowing how will set you free

What is stress? When I looked up the word stress, I found that there are many ways of defining stress. Stress has different meanings depending on who is defining it and for what purpose because many would find it difficult to define stress. Stress is nothing but a normal physiological response of the body to situations or stimuli that are perceived as "dangerous" to the body. Stress can affect anyone at anytime in life. When stress occurs regularly and is not dealt with, it causes the body to be on high alert, harming the body and its functions, emotions, mind, and spirit. I believe the word stress has and is being overused. It is one of those words that has become so commonly used that it covers a whole spectrum of emotions and feelings that follow when pressure is put on a person. We all assume that when someone says they are stressed that everyone is talking about the same thing as we are. I don't believe that to be so, unless we ask what they mean by stress.

A few years ago I visited the village I was partly raised in, and I asked one of the kids to get me a mango from the tree. She said, "Auntie you are stressing me out." I asked, "How am I stressing you? Her answer was, "You are taking me away from my playtime, and I don't really want to stop." Instead of just saying no. The word stress had a whole new meaning for me.

Here are some varying definitions of stress (From CoachingtoHappiness.com).

"Some researchers distinguish between Eustress and distress [Eustress is a term coined by endocrinologist Hans Selye which is defined in the model of Richard Lazarus (1974) as stress that is healthy, or gives one a feeling of fulfillment or other positive feelings. Eustress is a process of exploring potential gains.] and Distress [when something changes for the worse].

Others use stress to cover anxiety, by which I mean a fear of what may happen.

Others define stress as being "beyond the individual's ability to cope."

What comes first—stress or overwhelm (overwhelm is being overpowered, engulfed, or overcome by something)? Are you stressed or overwhelmed because you don't feel good enough about your job, what you do, your relationship, your looks, your shape, or you as a whole? The list goes on.

Some people believe that when we clearly define what stress really is, we are better able to understand it. Are we going to clearly define something that is as changeable as stress and are we as humans going to agree on one definition?

Does this mean that only when we understand stress, can we control, manage, and prevent it from happening? I don't believe that because of the variations of definitions of stress we will not agree on what it is.

For me the simple way to handle stress is to ask myself questions like these: What is putting pressure on me? How can I release the pressure? Stress is the bodily reaction and response to an emergency or difficult situations, a natural instinct that is embedded within all individuals in this world. A small dose of stress not only helps the body to function normally, but it also enables an individual to be more creative and efficient at work. This gives you insights to being your own coach. However, when stress becomes too much, and you have no coping tools; the body reacts little by little. Sooner or later it reacts in an extremely negative manner, leading to many different mental, emotional, and physical illnesses. The questions you alone can answer for yourself are how do I respond or react when I am under pressure or when something is stressing me? When I say I am stressed what do I mean?

Physical symptoms: What is experienced in physically?
There are many physical symptoms that are stress related. Here are some physical symptoms that can also be caused by other illnesses, so it is important to have a medical doctor check and treat conditions such as ulcers, compressed disks, or other physical disorders. Remember, however, that the body and mind are not separate entities. Some of the physical problems outlined below may result from or be exaggerated by stress or anything perceived as pressure. When you are not feeling good enough there is a tendency to not be aware of what your physical body may be telling you or sometimes we tend to ignore some of these symptoms. I often hear people say they thought it would go away. Someone said to me I don't want to waste the doctor's time.

Do you get any of these symptoms?

- sleep disturbances or sleepless nights
- back, shoulder, or neck pain
- tension or migraine headaches
- upset or acid stomach, cramps, heartburn, gas, or irritable bowel syndrome
- constipation or diarrhea
- weight gain or loss,
- hair loss
- muscle tension
- fatigue
- high or low blood pressure
- irregular heartbeat, palpitations
- asthma or shortness of breath
- chest pain
- sweaty palms or hands

- cold hands or feet
- skin problems (hives, eczema, psoriasis, tics, itching)
- periodontal disease or jaw pain
- reproductive problems
- immune system suppression: more colds, flu, infections
- growth inhibition and many more.

How many of the above relate to you or someone you know?

Emotional symptoms
Like physical signs, emotional symptoms such as anxiety or depression can mask conditions other than stress. It is important to find out whether they are stress related or not. In either case, the following emotional symptoms are uncomfortable and can affect your performance at work or play, your physical health, or your relationships with others. Again, a visit to your health care provider is encouraged when experiencing any of these symptoms or anything similar.

- nervousness, anxiety
- depression, moodiness
- butterflies
- irritability, frustration
- memory problems
- lack of concentration
- trouble thinking clearly
- feeling out of control
- substance abuse
- phobias
- overreactions
- and many more.

How many of the above relate to you or someone you know?

Relational symptoms

As I said before, all areas of your life can be affected by stress if not dealt with as soon as discovered or realized. How you relate to one another can put pressure on you, especially if you don't feel good about yourself.

Antisocial behavior can be present in stressful situations and can cause rapid worsening of relationships with family, friends, coworkers, your boss, or even strangers. Check with your health care provider if you are experiencing any of these signs and symptoms. A person under stress may show the following:

- increased arguments
- isolation from social activities
- conflict with coworkers or employers
- frequent job changes
- road rage
- domestic or workplace violence
- overreactions
- may become fearful of others and of things
- inner conflict or depression and many more.

How many of the above relate to you or someone you know?

In the course of my research, I found that when the economy went down, I noticed many news articles on domestic violence; most of these articles stated that domestic violence had increased. The conclusion I came to was that with the additional stress of people losing jobs, financial instability, and the overall economic recession, marital abuse rates are even higher than usual. Do you think when recession is on us, and a person loses his or her job he or she feels good about himself or herself, especially if they grew up not feeling good about themselves? How is the stress level in your own life at this time?

Chapter 3

Culture and Ancestory

A new word—*ancestory*

We all came from somewhere and we are connected to those who have gone before, our forefathers, and foremothers. What is culture? Here are a few definitions of culture from the Web:

* A particular society at a particular time and place; "example Mayan civilization"

* Their tastes in art and manners that are favored by a social group all the knowledge and values shared by a society.

Culture refers to the cumulative deposit of knowledge, experience, beliefs, values, attitudes, meanings, hierarchies, religion, notions of time, roles, spatial relationships, concepts of the universe, and material objects and possessions acquired by a group of people in course of generations through individual and group striving.

What Joseph Conrad says on biology resonates with what I think about humans being raised in the tribal or family medium just like the microorganism grows. "[Biology] the growing of microorganisms in a nutrient medium [such as gelatin or agar]; 'the culture of cells in a petri dish'" * polish: a highly developed state of perfection; having a flawless or impeccable quality; "They performed with great polish." —Joseph Conrad

Humans grow in a special preparation; "same as the biologist grows microorganisms."

The reason I am comparing Conrad's quote to human culture is, when a person is raised in a loving, compassionate, and caring culture medium, he/she grows to be a caring, loving, and compassionate individual. Perhaps he/she will have less of the inner conflict, because he/she grew up in a special preparation. Maybe he/she will have the attitudes and behavior that are characteristic of a particular social group or organization that raised them just like the microorganisms grown in a nutrient medium in a petri dish.

Here is a quote to illustrate more of what I am saying about one's culture and *ancestory*.

"There is no king who has not had a slave among his ancestors, and no slave who has not had a king among his." Helen Keller

We all came from somewhere. We all had a variety of enriching experiences, and we have many different lenses through which we attempt to make sense of our world and live our life purpose. At the end of the day, we have created our biography and time line and yet our daily experiences have altered who we thought we were at the beginning of the day. Our ancestors are what we are following and emulating consciously and unconsciously most of the time.

It doesn't matter what part of the world you are in as you read this book written by a Zimbabwe born author. I believe that my ancestral culture, beliefs, values and tradition were suppressed at some point in my life. I suppressed this rich tradition I was born in, because I wanted to be educated. My educators, for whatever reasons, where motivated to remove the African—including the culture, personality and tribal identity, values, and tradition—out of me and make me a black Christian with a white Christian mind. I am not saying that there is anything wrong with Christianity; I am saying the way it was done in those days was not very Christian. That is a story for another book. In a nutshell, I gave up my personal and cultural identity for intellectual education. In doing so, I stifled all my emotions in order to protect my heart and spirit. I am sure you know or have heard of many similar stories. Perhaps you may be someone who went through something like my experience. Timeline management will help you gain some insights to leverage into what is stopping you from becoming what you deeply want or dream of.

What is the outcome on your life from the experience? What is your story? Tell the story to yourself and find the lessons, growth, and bring out the jewel from within your life experience. Having been raised by two different cultures, I learnt that I need to respect both, keep my birth culture and learn and respect other people's culture and beliefs; I don't have to drop mine in order to learn the other.

On the surface I was a perfect person. I smiled a lot and was a caregiver and a caretaker. Inside, I was suffering. I was fighting conflicts, and I was angry and ashamed of whom I was. I felt guilty, and my spirit was dying a slow death. You name it—it was all crowded in me. Like my brother said to me once, "so angry inside that if I didn't drink, I could kill." I see things like drugs or alcohol used in excess as a coping mechanism to numb emotions like pain or anger. I used to see red when the stifled anger got the best of me, and I didn't have the guts to express what I was angry about.

In my culture, our ancestors play a big role in our lives. We don't necessarily worship them, but we respect them, honor them, trust them, and ask them for guidance and forgiveness. We create cultural rituals often, for many different reasons. When a child is born, the grandmother, who mostly is the midwife, would be the one who bathed the baby and then handed the baby to the mother for breastfeeding. The grandmother changes the diaper, literally taking care of the baby and performs traditional rituals.

Funerals are where all the different emotions are expressed in the open, no hiding there in the village because everything is done outside. Remember Africa is mostly warm weather except winter, and then a big bonfire is created, and everyone stands around the fire. Storytelling is a great way of learning about your ancestors, your forefathers, or those who have gone before. You do miss out in life when you don't ask questions of your heritage and where you came from. It helps you understand some of your quirks and why you look and behave the way you do. I believe some of these inadequacies or adequacies may have come from your grandfather or great-grandfather or grandmother. Part of my inheritance from my father's side of the family, is healing; my grandmother was a great healer, shaman, and herbalist, and I know and understand that now. I have come to embrace all that I have inherited from my *ancestory*. By doing so I am continuously surprising myself with what I discover is inside me. At the same time we do not have to get carried away by it all. It is wise to make sure that your ancestors' teaching and beliefs are still true for you. Ask yourself if you still believe, if they make sense to you, and if you want to continue following them.

It's like the story of the woman who breaks up the turkey's legs before she puts the bird in the oven. When asked by the husband why she breaks the turkey legs, her answer is, "My mother always did it."

The husband became curious and did research, asked the mother-in-law, and she said, "Oh, my mother always did it."

He went to the grandmother who also said. "Oh my mother always did it."

Fortunately the great-grandmother was still alive. When the old lady was asked why she broke the turkey legs, she said, "Oh, the pan was too small. I had to break the legs, so that it would fit in the pan."

Asking questions will get us the answers we need. Seek and you will find; ask and it shall be given. Knock and the door shall be opened. Trust yourself and ask for what you need to know. Some of you are saying, "All my elders are gone into the spirit world," meaning they are dead. This, I find to be the easiest thing to do. It doesn't cost you a penny—no long-distance charges. Call on your loved ones in spirit to answer some of your questions. "Okay," you are saying, "I can't do that. Are you crazy?" No, I am not crazy. As a medium, I do speak to spirits all the time; they want to communicate with us.

A few years ago I worked with a woman I will call Pat. Her mother had died, and they didn't really have a good relationship since Pat was a teenager. When she came to me for spiritual counseling, she was feeling guilty that she had never reconciled with her mother. During our session, I discovered the many emotions Pat had, and everything was all tangled up in this guilt and shame. We did what I now call spiritual/virtual forgiveness with Pat and her mother. All sorts of emotions like unacknowledged anger and resentment came up. It took a couple of hours. After the session she went home.

At the end of the day, I got a phone call from Pat. She was ecstatic. She could hardly speak from excitement, confusion, and all kinds of emotions. When she finally settled down what I remember is her saying, "When I got home, my phone rang. I noticed my mother's phone number on the display. I picked up the phone, and there was no one on the other side."

She also said she had a sense right there that her mother had forgiven her and felt that unconditional love had come into her, the love of a mother for her daughter. Here we are. This is a true story. They hear you, and they respond. Give it a try; it may take some time. If you have a loved one in the world of spirits, they want to hear from you, and you want to hear from them.

Let's learn from our culture and ancestors about ourselves. Let's learn from other people's cultures about them and how we can relate better. Most countries now have a diverse melting-pot culture; be interested, learn, and increase your knowledge of others. Why think that my culture is the only one and everyone needs to conform to it? No, that is now history. If you notice that someone is putting you and your culture down, be strong in yours. Let it exude from you that you believe in your own culture, in what God gave you, and that you and your culture are good enough and you are enough. You don't have to take on other people's culture.

Chapter 4
Your Life Story

What is your story? We humans are a moving storybook.

Let's look at when a child is born. Everyone goes "goo-goo ga-ga," and almost everyone says nice things about the new baby. It seems like that baby brings people into an inner place of peace, love, and joy. From that moment of birth, the child has begun his or her storybook. Even though it's a nonverbal story, it is a story the child will have for the rest of his or her life. As that child grows to become an adult, if he or she chooses, he or she can go back into his or her life story and experience the good, the bad, and the ugly. Those memories may be kept the same or he or she can rewrite, letting go of what he or she doesn't want.

I was raised on stories as is customary in my tradition, and my grandmothers were great storytellers. Visiting my time line from before birth to now, I am a storehouse of stories about the good, the bad, and the ugly. If it weren't for these stories I carry, relate, and tell out loud, I wouldn't be who I am now. When I tell my stories, especially those I have suppressed for a long time, they bring out a lot of emotions. They touch my heart and many other hearts to which I speak, and healing takes place.

Having been raised with so many conflicts, I was not congruent, meaning I wasn't who I made people believe I was—my words and action did not match. I found that I did not know or remember a lot of my life stories, and when I did they were mixed up. I believe this is due to suppressing my true feelings and all that happened in my life at different ages. When I began to share or speak out about some of my childhood experiences, I started to remember things and situations, and many feelings started to surface. Talk about a rollercoaster at times. But you know what? At the end of it all, I felt a lot better and lighter, and I began to almost like myself.

You might say, "I have no stories or I don't remember my childhood." I hear this lot in the spiritual counseling sessions and workshops I give. Nevertheless, when I share my own story or someone else's story, people start to come up with some of their own. I also suggest that they write some of what they remember of their life stories using what is developing right now in this life that they remember. Guess what? Other stories come to mind after the fact bit by bit.

In my experience, both personally and professionally, most of our stories continue to repeat themselves as we mature, in different flavors and ways. It is amazing to see how we keep repeating the same story with different actors, voices, and costumes. Watch your life. You will be surprised to see how many times you have been on the stage of your life with different actors and props but the same script. Chronological logic doesn't matter at all. It's what you get from the story, the lessons, and especially the emotions the story brings. This to me is the freeing of that part I have held hostage for however long. Inside each and every one of us there is something kicking and screaming, knocking somewhere within us saying, "Let me out of here." As I gain experience in freeing myself from the demons I have held deeply within me, I now want to focus my energy on helping others free themselves from similar or different demons or challenges that are asking to be freed. I can see the changes in me and in those I help. What is your life story?

Your story is worth repeating to yourself and to others. Guess what? There are people out there who will find your story to be very helpful, if not healing in itself. Tell your life story, your love story, or any story. It may not be a Hollywood hit movie or *New York Times* best seller, but it is your story, and no one can tell it better than you can. If you have kids or grandkids, they want to hear your life story. They want to hear what made you the person you are, how you met the person you married, what makes you happy or sad and where you got your wisdom.

Your body, your mind, your emotions, and spirit are ready to support you in your sharing especially if you tell those stories with emotions and conviction; you can harness an unbelievable healing power for you and those listening.

Client story
In my work starting as a nurse, then into makeup, and natural therapy, the ability to listen to people without judgment has been my biggest blessing. I hear many stories about clients' lives, how they grew up, their perceptions about what is real, and perhaps what happened during those younger years.

One of my favorites is Pinna, a young woman in her thirties, who was very stressed, on the run, and with her body screaming for help. When she started to tell me the edited version of her story, her body showed more pain, contraction, and not letting go of the discomfort.

According to Pinna, life was perfect. I asked a lot of questions and also listened to the words and tone of voice, to the body, the emotions, body language, and what was underneath the words. I asked her about what she likes doing as a hobby or for fun. Without missing a beat, she said playing violin. I asked, "Are you playing it these days?" Her body tensed up more, the tone of voice changed, and she said, "No, I don't have the time for that."

Pinna was very articulate and loved her three children very much. She said she was busy with work, housekeeping, and taking care of her husband and kids. I asked her another question with the intention of helping her do something for herself. I asked, "Could you take five minutes and play for your kids?" The answer came with a lot of emotion including, anger, resentment, and anger toward my suggesting that she play for her kids.

She said, "How dare you ask me to play for them? I am not good enough." What I got was how could I ask her to do something she loves when she has these duties and obligations to her family and job. Playing a violin was not important to them.

She then said she wasn't a professional, meaning she was not good enough to play for her kids. Why would she want to put them through that? I feel she shortchanged herself. Kids are a great audience for a short period of time. She said I wasn't being compassionate by suggesting a five-minute concert for an audience that already thinks she is a great mum. A great mum who does all she does for them; a mum who loves her kids so much that she gives up her favorite hobby to spend more time providing for them. I think Pinna is the best mum for those kids, and playing for them would let her become the best mum for her own inner kid.

Your story is waiting. It's about you and your life. What you have seen, experienced, and lived is important to you and to the rest of us. You don't have to be a great storyteller. The stories want to come out; they don't want to be locked in the prison of our minds, our hearts, and mostly our bodies. Tell the story, and it will set you free. The more you allow the story to tell itself, the more the not feeling good about yourself will slowly disappear.

I know in reflexology, which is a specialized foot massage, they say "stories your feet can tell." Yes, feet have stories to tell. Can you imagine with your whole body, mind, emotions, and spirit, how big and elaborate the story could be? You don't have to write a book about it. Just tell it as you feel it.

One of my stories is about being in nursing school and how most student nurses who had experienced my stories wanted to hang around me at breaks. I asked someone, "Why is it that everyone wanted to go to breaks with me?" She said, "Because you are very funny, and your stories are hilarious, inspiring, and have meaning."

You know what? I had no idea and I had never thought that way about stories, my humor, and myself. As I grew up, that part of my life story was off my radar until recently. As I began to reinvent myself, several people have reminded me how funny I was and how they love to hear my stories. Going back in time and visiting my time line, I found my funny parts and I am embracing them. Embrace yours. I give you 100 percent permission to embrace every part of who you are. YOU don't need my PERMISSION. Give yourself the permission you need to bring out that part that has been locked up.

Somehow we seem to think we need someone else's permission to have fun; I think it's because as kids we had to ask our parents or those who raised us to go and play, so we are still operating from that place in time. Give yourself the permission you need. All you need is for you to give yourself the permission to tell your story, have fun, and be silly. Give it a try and you may find healing in your story.

Chapter 5

INVISIBLE SUPPORT AND GUIDES

Do you know that you live a double life? You are here in the physical world where you have a body, and you are also in the energy world or the spirit world—the invisible world.

There is an invisible world out there; the world seen only by those who have allowed their inner sight to support them and for those who just trust that these trusted helpers are not in our material world where we have to pay money for their services. We don't pay this invisible support system, but they are waiting to be asked to help. You, I, and everyone else are all in the world of duality. We talked about your ancestors in Chapter 3 and how they desperately want to connect and support you. They want to see you succeed, even though they are now no longer here in the physical world, you cannot see them, and they cannot hold your hand.

Think of some invisible encounters you have had or heard about. Come on, you are not weird to believe in the unseen world. Even Hollywood is making movies about the unseen.

Depending on the faith in which you were raised or what you believe in now, this will let you know whether you believe or not in this vast world of spirits. Yes, to quote Munroe, "we are more than our physical body."

If you believe or not, do a little experiment. Sit in a comfortable place, relax, take a few deep breaths, close your eyes, and continue with the breathing. If you are still at ease, connect to the deepest place within you. This place is like coming home to yourself. You will know when you are there.

This will take some practice. Even the relaxation itself takes practice; so don't be disappointed if it doesn't happen right away. Once you are in that place, your center, your home, ask for, say, a loved one who is in spirit—a grandparent, an angel to perhaps talk to, say something, ask a question, ask to be given a feeling, a word, a sensation, a touch—anything that will let you know it is someone nonphysical.

This may sound hokey, spooky, weird or whatever to some of you. But if you are reading this book, you must be looking for something different in your life. Allow yourself to go outside the box to see what the instructions say because the content of the box is written on the outside. The more you practice, the easier and more believable it becomes.

First time I asked my spirit people to give me a physical sign, I asked them for the sign to be flowers; the next day a client brought me a blooming Easter lily. This person had never done this before; she said to me as she was coming to her appointment, she was compelled to stop at the market and buy me flowers. She bought the blooming lilies because the flowers would last longer.

Some of you may be saying, "Yeah, right." How do you know I am not making it up? In my world, making it up is okay; it is your practice. Fake it 'til you make it.

Now that you have experienced having a visit, you can actually talk to your loved ones anytime. Your ancestors, your guides, your angels—anything you believe in is waiting to talk and help you. In the book *Conversations with God* by Neale Donald Walsch, these kinds of conversations with God, Spirit, or anyone in the spirit world are no different than having a conversation with your friend and relatives here on earth. It doesn't matter what you think people will think and say about you.

Why do you care? Do you suffer from the condition called Not Good Enoughsitis? It's a new condition I have found to very common in mankind.

I read a book titled *What You Think of Me Is None of My Business* by Whittaker Cole. I don't remember much of the content, and I am not even sure if I actually finished reading the book. I was taken by the titleo I use this all the time when I am regressing back into my old pattern of *not good enoughsitis*. Really, what anybody thinks of you or you of them is none of your or their business. People are always thinking and saying something about somebody or something. You cannot do anything about someone else's thoughts or action.

I have discovered over the years that people are not comfortable with something they don't see or with the shadow or the darkness. Somehow, somewhere, someone decided that intangible, unseen darkness is bad, so let's be scared of it. Why is that? I have no idea. Maybe it is not being secure or comfortable in the something we consider bad. Because you can't hold it in your hands or see it with your physical eyes, it is what we call bad. I have also heard that the unseen, the darkness is evil. If God created everything, how could anything be evil?

The unseen world is alive and pulsating with life and energy, and we are welcomed by it and in it.

Is there any negative energy out there? Remember the natural law of opposites, the law of attraction? The polarity lives with us, and it is the law, so get over it. What do you want to attract—positive or negative? If you attract positive, what is on the other side of it? We live in the world of duality—good and bad, right and left, night and day, and the list goes on. Keep your mind focused on what you want. What has your life been about up to this point?

Unconsciously some parts of my life were marred by some of my negative thought, feelings, fears about the unseen world, beliefs, and especially the belief that I wasn't good enough. I felt those in the spirit world would not be interested in helping me. When I chose to look at and explore deep within to see what negative thoughts I had about myself and what I was capable to doing and being, my life began to change. I began to delve into communicating with the unseen world. Guess what? They responded.

Make a choice, and you have given yourself permission to attract what you want to contact. Have you seen the movie *The Secret?* If you have, then you would know what I am talking about. *The Secret* talks about natural laws that I am talking about; there is a lot more to natural law that we miss out on. Always obey and respect the natural laws—think of the law of attraction and the law of gravity. There are many natural laws out there that are not made by any human beings or any government of your or my country or any country for that matter. The Golden Rule is another example of natural law, and it is found in almost all religions. Humanism teaches the Golden Rule as follows: the Golden Rule is an ethical code that states one has a right to justice, therefore do unto others what you would like them to do unto you. Doing unto others that which you do to yourself is what we do. Unfortunately, we sometimes treat ourselves badly, and we take that example of treatment to others. Others see how we treat ourselves, and they treat us the same way.

When we are afraid of spirits and the unseen world, we are not doing justice to those who live in it, and we are not doing justice to our own spirit, which really could use some help, to learn and fulfill its purpose here on earth. Understanding and working with these natural laws will help you explore this unseen world.

The *spirit world,* according to *spiritualism,* is the world inhabited by spirits. Though a concept of a spirit world is in the constitution of most religions, it is not itself the religion. Though independent from the physical world, both the spirit world, and the physical world are in constant interaction.

Yes, spirit lives; you can connect and work with those in the spirit world. The spirit world is part of the natural law. This may sound hokey or like hocus-pocus.. Well, you will soon learn to stay open. Like the saying goes, the mind is like a parachute—it works best when open. Keep an open mind, and all will work out for you. I am not saying keep your parachute open and invite in anything and everything. Skydivers do not keep their chutes open all the time. Go and learn about connecting with the spirit world. You might surprise yourself.

I recall a lady I'll call Mona. She once told me, "Guess what? I have all these spirits who hung around me last week driving to Toronto [Canada]. My car was full with many spirits." She looked spacey, not there or with it, and one thing that I really saw in her was that she was carrying a different energy than I normally saw in her. I asked Mona if she knew who these spirits were. She said, "No." I told her to go home, open all her windows and doors, and invite anyone to come in. Her response was, "Are you crazy? I don't want anybody or strangers to come into my house. What if they steal my stuff? People I don't know coming into my house? No way." I then explained to her that she was leaving all her energy doors and windows open for anyone to come in.

Remember your spiritual doors, windows, and parachute need not stay open for everyone to come in. Have a sign that reads, "By invitation only." And have a doorkeeper. These are some of the things you learn when you want to start opening up to the world of spirit and its energies. There are a lot of courses given, so find yourself a well trained medium or intuitive with whom to train. Look for someone whose teachings resonate with you.

Where is spirit? Spirit is about and around us, meaning everywhere in the invisible world. Wherever you are, spirit is there, too. You don't have to go far looking for spirit.

The only thing you need is to look at yourself and your desire to connect with that world of the invisible, the world that wants to help you and also wants to learn and grow with you.

When we are feeling good about ourselves we tend to want to explore, we are not afraid to try new things. Feeling good about yourself will give you the courage to connect with the spirit world and develop a relationship with your loved ones and helpers.

Chapter 6
EMOTIONS

The E word is a word not too many people want to be associated with. There are people I call *the emotions associated* and *the emotions dissociated*.

Which one are you? I am not saying those who are associated with their emotions are emotional. I am not saying those who are dissociated are unemotional. I am saying know your emotions and be comfortable with them and in them. Emotions are a part of being human. If you don't recognize them, they are running and/or ruining your life. Emotion is energy in motion.

Okay, beating around the bush is not my style. Let's be open and honest with each other. Emotions are the fuel that gets you moving. Have you ever been angry or seen someone angry, and then they take anger to action? Watch out! They can be very productive. Emotions, if allowed, will make you take action. Sometimes when I am angry and I allow myself to channel that energy to take action, I can do all the chores I have been procrastinating about and have them done in no time. And the anger will have lessened.

How do you deal with your emotions like anger?
Write it down here.

One of my favorite quotes is *"You'll never understand the reason, until you look deep enough into the cut to see the emotional pain that put it there" (C.L. Bartholdi).*

Most people are suffering from a lot of unresolved issues, old business, stifled emotions, negative feelings, or issues that have been pushed back into the psyche, mind, and body. It's all there—some visible and some invisible to the eye or to the person carrying them.

Have you or someone you know been to see your doctor complaining of pain, and all test results are negative, but the pain is still there? The doctor says you are in very good health, not to worry, and everything will be all right. Or the doctor says there is nothing wrong with you. Or perhaps you are given a prescription of some drug to help kill the pain. I see drugs as medicating the pain and pushing down what is really bothering you; maybe the drug helps to mask the pain or maybe not.

Emotional pain is intangible, but sometimes it actually causes physical pain, and there is nothing visible on all the tests. Yes, visit your health care provider and follow his/her suggestion, but at the same time, be part of the solution.

Here are some Canadian statistics from Stats Canada. In 2003, Canadians spent $15 billion on prescription drugs a year, an increase of 14.5 percent over 2002. Can you imagine what the numbers are for 2011 and what they will be by 2020? People take these pills like candies. Do your own statistics about what you are taking. Maybe do your own fact-finding. Ask your friends or relatives if they are taking medication, maybe anti-depressants or painkillers. I am not saying don't take pills prescribed for you; I am saying check in to see why you are in pain or depressed or whatever it is that is troubling you. See your counselor, your spiritual director, or your spiritual leader and, of course, your medical doctor.

Like I said before, emotion is energy in motion. When it gets trapped and is not allowed to move like it's meant to, it starts to talk to the trapper. It talks using the body where unfortunately it is trapped. Over time it becomes something, like a physical condition or a disease—a chronic one for that matter. It becomes incurable, and the end result is not what you want.

I have spent most of my adult life in North America working in the health and healing profession, and I have witnessed how the majority of my fellow citizens are in touch or should I say rooted with their intellectual side and not deeply connected to their emotions. When I say "deeply," I mean going into the core. It is more like an intellectual connection to the emotional department.

In my practice it has been a rare honor to have someone bless me with his or her raw emotions. Some of them, upon discovering their raw emotions, have directed them at me - their helper -or those near and dear to them.

I remember one incident when this man came to see me because someone had suggested that I could help him discover where his emotions lived. I asked him if he was sure he wanted to go there. He said "yes" and assured me it was time; he was tired of suffering inside. Well, to make this story short, he did get there, and it was primitive and painful. It was a blessing to witness.

But I guess because he had lived an intellectual emotional life, when he got home and back into his head and the emotional healing experience didn't make sense, I received a verbal accusatory phone call, saying, "You are not a good therapist. You made me so angry, and you don't know what you are doing. I want my money back."

I did refund the money. For me it is not about the money; it's about taking personal responsibility, ownership, and saying, "Yes, I have been holding on to anger. I am glad I have started to release most of it, and I want to heal my life of any emotions I hold such as anger. I want a happy life. Life is very short, and we are running out of time to heal our lives. As we mature and age, it is time to make those healing choices and take personal responsibility. If you believe in reincarnation, then doing some healing means that when you come back, you won't have to deal with the same issues. Do you want to come back into your next life and face the same people and the same issues such as not feeling good enough about yourself? Not me.

Happiness, joy, and love are not caused by events but by our attitude. We can learn to choose how we want to feel. Why not choose love and joy? Heal what is blocking all the love, joy, and happiness. Reading *The Course in Miracles*, I truly understand why I do what I do—helping people heal. I am paraphrasing: "We spent our lifetime looking for love. Instead we should spend the time looking for what is blocking the love we seek, because love is always there." This is what my work is all about. I hope in this book I am doing the same, helping you discover why you are unhappy, sad, or angry and looking for love, joy, happiness, and whatever it is you seek or is missing in your life when it is already within you. Work on finding and releasing the blocks. Love and joy will fill you because love is all around. Love is like oxygen, which is always present all around. All we have to do is allow it in. Most of all remember that you are love and you are loved.

Here are some soul-searching thoughts that I find engaging by Walter Last, in spiritual philosophy of science (Web site www.heal-yourself.com.au).

In his article "The World of Feelings and Emotions," he offers this food for thought:

"We all would like to live a happy, healthy, and fulfilled life, yet few seem to be able to do just that. Why must we have so much suffering, failures, and disappointments? We just want to be secure in a loving relationship and a satisfying job with a good income and enjoy ourselves."

I add why do we spend so much of our energy telling ourselves that we are not good enough? Why do we spend so much time carrying and holding on to the blocks and wounds of the past?

Take some time to ponder and answer these questions for yourself. Be aware of anything that comes up for you during your reading and writing feel what is coming up acknowledge it in any way you feel comfortable in doing. Your body mind is continuously letting you know what is really going on. Take the time to do just that; listen and write a little more about what you are discovering.

Chapter 7
THE HUMAN BODY

Body of a human: The Human Machine
I found this reference on the body to be very interesting. How many people see, think, and use the body as was viewed by René Descartes in 1640? Give this a read and come up with your own conclusion about how you honestly view "your body"—how you treat it, use it, or perhaps abuse it.

This is a description of the human body from Wikipedia:

"The Description of the Human Body from MedlinePlus (*La description du corps humain*) is an unfinished treatise written in the 1640s by René Descartes. Descartes felt knowing oneself was particularly useful. This for him included medical knowledge. He hoped to cure and prevent disease, even to slow down aging.

"René Descartes believed the soul caused conscious thought. The body caused automatic functions like the beating of the heart and digestion he felt. The body was necessary for voluntary movement as well as the will. However, he believed the power to move the body be wrongly imagined to come from the soul. A sick or injured body does not do what we want or moves in ways we do not want. He believed the death of the body stopped it from being fit to bring about movement. This did not necessarily happen because the soul left the body.

"René Descartes believed the body could exist through mechanical means alone. This included digestion, blood circulation, muscle movement, and some brain function. He felt we all know what the human body is like because animals have similar bodies and we have all seen them opened up.

"He saw the body as a machine. He believed the beat of the heart somehow caused all movement of the body. Blood vessels he realized were pipes; he saw that veins carried digested food to the heart. (This was brought further by William Harvey. Harvey developed the idea of the circulation of the blood.) Descartes felt that an energetic part of blood went to the brain and there gave the brain a special type of air imbued with vital force that enabled the brain to experience, think, and imagine. This special air then went through the nerves to the muscles enabling them to move."

I wonder what the science world said then about the above. They may have said something like this: "It is a remarkable mixture of advanced thought ahead of our time, which is just speculation—unproved, unsound." And the science of today's world would call it unscientific with no research to back up his claim.

What do you say? Remember you are your own scientist who is exploring how you work.

Here is a story of a person who held a lot of turmoil inside.

When P.J., a single man in his fifties and an engineer, was told he had HIV, a hush-hush condition, P.J. became depressed and angry; he had thoughts of suicide or wishing he could just disappear. He was faced with the most difficult decision he ever had to make. He had never tried anything other than allopathic medicine. He wasn't about to tell his family and friends, as in those days he would have been shunned. He went into a bout of all sorts of emotions, just like a roller coaster.

The illness snowballed into AIDS, and he became weak. The torment was visible on his face and body. He had kept so many secrets to himself all his life. After meeting me, he told me, "Chipo, you don't take BS from anyone." I agreed. He asked me for a healing, and I said he had to be prepared to face his inner torment that he had been suppressing. I said, "No projection" (meaning that he was not to blame me or anyone else for the feelings that could come up). I could see how much emotional pain he was holding.

By the end of our one-and-one-half-hour session, he had some major releases of unfinished business that needed to be addressed. Healing one's past is very important in healing the soul that came here to heal, learn, transform, and return home with something to show on its report card.

How does one choose between an old lie that now is eating you inside, a life full of lies to everyone, and your spirit that is ready to heal or just die?

Can the secret(s) continue to live? Or can P.J. continue to keep the secret he had been keeping for years without it destroying himself and everyone in his wake?

His world was falling apart right before his eyes, and there was nothing out there to take the feelings away or help except himself. He found himself acting in ways he could not even begin to understand. When his internal struggles turned to dangerous behavior, even the paranormal connection he shared with a handful of friends who could tolerate his behavior was not enough to save him.

P.J. delved into the journey of self-discovery through shamanic healing work, and he felt emotions intellectually. It slowly was heartfelt, and his exploring of the depth of his soul's desire was fulfilling to him.

Sometimes my healer grandmother would take in people who needed more support in their healing process to live in her home. I followed this model with P.J. He lived in my house for a month. This experience taught me more than I realized about myself and about a person who is suffering inside. I learned that an inner tormented person could get his/her world very mixed up just like cream of soup and that world could be scrambling down with them and if you, the outsider helper, buy into the person's story and behavior, and take it all personally or allow what is coming up from the person to affect and infect you, you have now become part of the problem. P.J. taught me how to not take someone's behavior as if it were my fault or take it personally. This also reminded me why my nursing tutors and teachers taught us not to get involved with our patients at the emotional level. That taught me detachment.

Explore your inner closets as honestly as you can and explore any secret(s) you hid from yourself and your world, and that maybe tormenting your inner being. Maybe it is time to say it out loud to yourself or to write it down. If you have a trusted friend, partner, or relative you can confide in, perhaps you could share what's coming up with him/her. Your healthcare provider may be the person to go to if they are into counseling. Take some time to explore and write down in the space provided or in your journal.

Even though some of us take the body or our whole being for granted or as a machine that takes us from point A to B, sooner or later it will speak up and make us listen and pay attention.

Some people are known to take better care of their cars than their physical bodies. Are you one of them? I hope not. If you are, I am glad you are reading this book. I hope that by the end of it you will have changed your thinking about your body and yourself, the only earthly vehicle you have in this life. I see the physical body as a shock absorber that takes and keeps everything; I mean everything that comes its way. Think about this. It takes any information and remembers it all until it's asked to let go.

I once had a poster in my office of a very old wrinkled face. The words at the bottom said, "If I knew I was going to live this long, I would have taken better care of myself." How are you treating your body?

Imagine this: one day you wake up as usual, your eyes refuse to open, your feet refuse to get out of bed, your whole body says, "Sorry, I am not getting out of bed today. I am on strike." Everything that is part of the body refuses to do any of their normal functions. What would you do? Scary thought!

I have heard stories similar to this where someone's body ached all over, and they were bedridden. Remember chronic fatigue syndrome when it hit the world? Chronic fatigue syndrome (CFS) is a disorder that causes extreme body and mind fatigue. You become very tired. This fatigue is not the kind of tired feeling you get after working hard and goes away after you rest or sleep. Instead, it lasts a very long time, even if you take a holiday. All you do is sleep. It limits your ability to do your normal mundane daily activities.

Some of the symptoms of CFS (symptoms meaning what the person suffering from it notices) are extreme fatigue that lasts anywhere up to six months or more and other problems such as low stamina, weakness, muscle pain, memory problems, headaches, multiple joint pains, depression, sleep disruption, sore throat, and a sluggish lymphatic system that may cause tenderness in the lymph nodes and hypersensitivity. Since other illnesses can cause similar symptoms, it is hard for a physician to diagnose. Usually the cause is unknown, and it was commonly found in women in their 40s and 50s; nevertheless, anyone else can have it. Well, if you pay attention to yourself and your body, maybe you can prevent this. Read the meditation part of this book. This insidious condition can last for years. Even after you are feeling better, it can creep back into your system. Attention and self-care is the key. Listen to your body.

Medicine says there is no medical cure for CFS, so the goal of treatment is to improve or maybe alleviate the symptoms. If you think you may have something similar, visit your medical doctor, do your own research, and look and incorporate some complementary modalities. I am not saying its just one way or this modality is the only one; as a healer it's my responsibility to remind you that you have choices. Don't just take my word for it—explore many avenues that resonate with you. You have many choices. In my school of thought, it's not "either/or" it is "this and that." Remember, I said put a team to work in your healing process, but be the CEO of taking care of your body, mind, emotions, and spirit. It is you who lives in these conditions twenty-four/seven, not them.

Remember the body remembers everything it has experienced; it is like a sponge that takes it all in and keeps it until told to let go. When the body has taken and kept all the different experiences good, or not so good, one starts to experience some discomfort and perhaps this becomes chronic meaning it is there all the time and a *dis-ease* of some kind surfaces. The discomfort may prevent you from functioning normally, and one may experience pain; if this persists, one may find they don't really feel good or happy, and this may lead to not feeling good enough about yourself. All these different issues that arise in the body may cause the person to go and seek medical help. Since the pain has manifested in the physical body, the doctor may offer different labels and treatment.

Another condition similar to CFS is Fibromyalgia syndrome, (FMS), which is pain everywhere in the body, generalized muscular pain, and fatigue. It usually affects the entire body, although it may start in one area such as the neck and shoulders, and it then spreads to other areas over a period of time. *Fibro* means muscle. *Myalgia* means pain in a muscle or in multiple muscles and the fibrous and connective tissues (the ligaments and tendons). Always remember that the body holds on to any suppressed emotions and experiences, negative or positive.

Many people suffered from, conditions like these and some still do. Could this be the body's way of saying I am tired or is the body going on strike? What is the warning your body giving you? I had you imagine what it might do. The body is a great machine that needs you as much as much as you need it; the more you love and take care of it, the more it will take great care of you. You have heard stories of people who have lived to be over one hundred-years-old and still functioned like a younger person if not better. I think they took care of themselves. What does it take to take care of your "body house"? It takes commitment not to anyone else but to you. I call it a "body house" because it houses your soul, spirit, mind, emotions, and the unknown. If you love your body and you feel good enough about your body, take care of it.

How do you take care of your house? Here are some strategic ideas that if kept in check, will help you keep your body in check. I am not going into details in this book; there is a lot already written about these subjects. Check your library.

Ask yourself this: How am I taking care of myself in all these areas of my life?

Use the scale of one to ten; one being not so good and ten being I am doing awesome.

- Nutrition
- Personal Grooming
- Physical Fitness
- Mental Grooming/Fitness
- Emotional Hygiene
- Psychological updates
- Spiritual Fitness

Add your own areas. Keeping all these in check and in your awareness at all times is a must if you want to really feel good about yourself. Start with one small thing at a time. It takes practice and patience.

Chapter 8
Spirit and Soul

The English word *spirit* has many different meanings and connotations but commonly refers to a supernatural being or essence—transcendent and therefore metaphysical in its nature. It is not a religion—it's the nature of who you are, and it relates to where we came from.

The Concise Oxford Dictionary defines spirit as "the nonphysical part of a person." Some people see *spirit* as another name for soul. Spirit is a natural part of our being. Others may identify spirit with mind, with consciousness, or with the brain or something out of their reach. What is your definition of spirit and of soul? I think it depends on the faith you were raised in and your belief system.

Here are my very short primitive definitions of spirit and soul:

Spirit is the God essence; the Creator essence not contaminated by the human stuff. I was taught that I was created in the image of God our Creator, hence I/you have inherited spirit identity.

Soul is both of God essence and of the personality and human essence coming here on earth with an agenda to learn, grow, and transform, and returning back to spirit with knowledge and understanding of the self.

When we start to delve into the spirit and soul, I find that like everything on the planet, everyone and every faith has their own description or definition and understanding. This is a great thing. I feel that we need to give each other space for our own understanding, taking it in, and digesting and assimilating it. Look at how many languages are spoken on earth.

Feed your soul and spirit healthy nutritious foods, and it will serve you well. When it comes to food for your spirit and soul, use what you grew up with, the spiritual food that raised you, unless like many other people you were turned off by the faith. Then, find something that nourishes you now and continue to explore.

Here is my old story about the confusion I had growing up with two opposites faiths and beliefs one very negative about others' beliefs and traditions, and the other faith okay with what was said by others' beliefs and teachings.

I was considered shy and reserved during my childhood years, and at the same time I was also seen as outgoing, outspoken, and friendly. Maybe I portrayed these mixed energies or messages just like the adults around me. When I look back, I don't think I was shy at all. I think I was reserved because I could not speak my mind, and I couldn't stand up to the people who were confusing and confused about their own lives.

I have had many life challenges with people who were not consistent and who didn't walk their talk. I have gotten past being challenged by inconsistency as I realize that one of my karmic or life lessons is to accept people as they are, including myself. I used to withdraw when I sensed that a person was not authentic—meaning not being genuine or sincere and truthfulness of origins, attributions, commitments, sincerity, and intentions was not being demonstrated. Earlier in my life, I would get angry, frustrated, and conflicted inside, not express myself, and at times, lash out. I did keep a lot of feelings inside for fear of being reprimanded, punished, or having something withheld from me, like my education.

Growing up receiving mixed messages from both family and educators around me was no fun. I got mixed up, and I also gave out mixed messages. What goes in must come out. These mixed messages included everything from who is God, to why I couldn't play with other kids who were non-Catholic or white, or why Jewish or Russian people were bad people, and we had to pray for them. I kept questioning and could not believe or trust what I was being told.

I was very skeptical. I now realize that perhaps I was wiser than my educators, and I was more accepting than they were. The more accepting idea led to inner conflict and confused stories. Abiding by the rules and not rocking the boat resulted in becoming very cynical of others and the world at large, especially those who gave the mixed messages. Is there something in your younger self that you can recall that made you skeptical, cynical or even out right angry or mad or happy and joyful? Revisit your time line again and see what is coming up. What sustained you when you were growing up?

Having been born with more melanin than the ruling population was not to my benefit. Actually it was costly and caused me to lose my inner freedom, personal identity, and faith in humanity. I think all this added to the inner and outer conflicts I was experiencing. Given all the war going on inside, there was another very strong, trusting, wise self that I was listening to; this something within was my saving grace.

Even though I was busy fighting for my outer freedom instead of connecting to that inner sensitivity and all the mixed emotions, the faith I felt within helped me to stay sane and to trust in something bigger than my outer world. I didn't know what that was at the time. I knew deep within myself that some guiding force was there for me, and I trusted it immensely.

My parents, especially my mother, had a very strong faith in God. Mother always said, "If God is willing, I will see you tomorrow" or "God will take care of this or that." In the regime I was born and grew up in, I did not have the freedom to express that inner faith and strength freely in order to do what I wanted or to move about freely. I left the country in search of outer freedom.

I never felt like a free person. I always felt like I was walking on glass or eggshells that should not be broken, so I trod lightly. When I started to work on myself, my life began to change. I began to want to change how I felt about myself. The feelings of not trusting others and myself started to become obvious; I did not feel good enough. I even doubted the aspect of myself that always guided me. What about you? Are you ready for that change you seek? I know you are, and you are good enough to want to bridge your feelings and your thoughts.

I started questioning what I had been told and taught as a youngster. Now I see how valueless I saw myself in my younger life, especially how I would feel scared of anything and everything, imagining that it or they were going to get me. I had so many fears in me that I would freeze when there was conflict. I imagined that I was the only one who felt this way, but now I have a different perception. I know I am not alone. Many people have similar feelings and thoughts about themselves. I believe we are all carrying excess luggage that is costing us a lot in our life, work, and relationships, and may be preventing us from carrying on our life purpose.

Looking back, I can laugh at some of what I feared, such as passing by a police station or seeing a police car I would shake and start to sweat. The old history from the old country was in me. I had to learn that the police force in Canada was not the same as in my birth country. One of the ways I decided to cure my fear of the police was to volunteer in a community program that involved the police.

Do you ever wonder how your friends or classmates you had as a child turned to be? We come from different backgrounds we all were raised differently perhaps family siblings raised by the same parents may turn out very differently.

Now that I have been examining myself and my life, and realizing that I am in charge of how I feel about my me I could do something about it and my life. I know that every person is responsible for the outcomes of their life, and with a little help, those stifled emotions can shift. My intention and focus now is to help people everywhere, especially those from my birth homeland, Zimbabwe. I wonder how I can assist them to come from where I was then to where I am now within myself. I wonder if most of these people feel the way I felt. Are they affected just like I was by their upbringing? I also wonder what are they thinking or feeling, and what is going on within their psyches and lives. I wonder if they were to look at what is happening around them, could they see a parallel with what is happening within them?

If only they could release some of those pent-up emotions and state what it is they felt and are still feeling, maybe forgive, understand, and let go, perhaps they would be able to go on with a different life. I would like to find out from them what choices they are making on their own and what responsibility they are taking for what is happening around them. From there I would like to share with the world what I have learned and experienced, and the solutions I have discovered what may help them in their lives. I want to create a movement encouraging those in the Diaspora (those who left their country of origin) to go back and help change their original community. The spirit and soul of our original is what created us and made us who we are.

As I look back at my life, I can see that education, religion, respecting and being kind to others, and not speaking back to your elders except in agreement because elders know what's best for you was what was encouraged. You had to do as you were told, "do as I say and not as I do," conforming to the rules and regulations, or else you were punished or kicked out of school. A child's own feelings, thoughts, and opinions were never considered to be important.

Having said that, children were loved and cared for dearly. A child was considered everyone's child and was looked after by everybody.

All that said and done, I have grown to be a better human being from all of my experience. My past helped to shape who I am today. Within all the inner confusion and conflict, I learned about the unseen world of spirit from my paternal grandmother and my native tradition, which I practiced underground. I now realized what a blessing that was to have some understanding of this world without fear. The unseen, intangible world is present even though it's not tactile like our familiar physical world. Let us connect to it, and let's appreciate that world using our other senses.

I am sure you have had some paranormal experiences of some type or help that came from nowhere. I believe we do have "spiritual" blind spot or side that makes us limited by our physical apparatus, blinding us to the true nature of who we really are and the existence of other realities willing to share this life.

Let's imagine for a moment that somehow, some miracle has happened. Our human blind spot is no longer there, and we can believe, know, and see what we couldn't see before. The veil has been lifted. That nonphysical perceptual sense accompanying our soul's identity is not only valid, true, and believable by us, it is also essential for our living here on the planet now. Here you can see everything you have never seen before.

Have you seen the movie *Pleasantville*, a 1998 film featuring Toby McGuire and Reese Witherspoon? It's a funny movie that touches on what I am saying. Lifting the veil will help us reach that higher level of consciousness of remembering who we really are, which is the true nature of our spirit. Remember we are spirit first, in the physical body, here on earth to learn, grow, and become our very best.

Why do we see or find ourselves groping or groaning in the dark side of our making? What is your thought on this? My theory is that it is because of our human blindness or refusal to open our consciousness to the higher levels of our natural or spiritual reality and the multidimensional experiences and expressions of our authentic/true selves waiting for us to return to and retain it forever. Take some time to pause and do some soul and spirit searching about your paranormal experiences and write about them.

It seems like we are not open to options. We have already won the power of our birthright, not through fear and manipulation like how I was raised. Days of using fear to make people comply with your teachings and not allowing them to have a voice of their own. Those days are over. Thank God.

Once I realized that there was a spiritual blind spot, my inner eyes started to want to open and see. Did they open instantly? No, they opened slowly, and they are still opening. It is like wiping the sleep from my eyes in the morning. I then realized that these people I blamed for my inner torture were my mirror. They were teachers who had a huge message for me to wake up to and begin healing myself. I started to look for the reasons I was born and began to let my light shine. I also realized that as a darker person, my light is intense. This light does affect people in different ways because the intensity is overwhelming for some, including me. One of the things I learned and practiced was to retrieve myself from that place of not feeling good about myself, and the not good enoughness changed into I am good enough for me." Are you ready to know what I learned? Drum roll please: "BREATHE". Yes, breath is life. If you are not breathing, you are dying. When you were born, and you took your first breath, you made the doctor or midwife, especially your mother, happy. Why? Because you were alive. Let's say you did not take that first breath. The doctor or midwife had to give a pat on your backside, shake you, or if worse came to worst, they were trained to help you breathe. Breath is life; breathing saves lives, and it changes lives. How many times have you heard the expressions "take a deep breath" and or "breathe from your diaphragm"? Do you know how to take a deep breath? Try this short exercise. This can be done seating in a comfortable chair or on the floor or lying on your back. (It is easier at the beginning to lay on your back to develop the proper deep breathing technique the first couple of Times. Put one hand on your upper chest and the other on your abdomen (belly)

- Take a deep Breath in slowly through your nose.
- Feel the hand on your abdomen rise.
- Breathe out slowly through your mouth. The hand on your belly should gradually lower. -Imagine a balloon in your abdomen that you are blowing up and then pushing the air out as you breathe out.

Repeat these steps few times. Notice how your ribcage expands and widen as your belly moves out, allowing your lungs to fill up. You don't need to breathe like this all the time.

I hope that we collectively have learned from our past, and we can continue to learn, grow, and evolve. I hope that we can raise and teach our children an open spirituality where they can learn about everything they can and make their own choices.

I am not so sure if we see that we can continue to treat each other with compassion, curiosity, and wonder. The good news is that the universe is evolving, as it should, whether we like it or not. Even though we are not quite there yet, I believe we are working our way to catch up. I believe that the unconscious or hidden collective intention is programmed to grow the soul's reality, perspective, and lessons to become its authentic self- while on this planet and in this physical vehicle, the body.

The time is NOW for self, the soul seeking or searching that will lead to self soul seeing, self soul knowing, self soul understanding and healing. Take action to accomplish this. Let each and every person find his or her own personal truth through direct experience and exploration of the inner environment, which will manifest into the physical. Be an example, be the leader of self-development, and you don't have to be a preacher. Just show the world the new you through your actions. We all know that trying to convert or change others does not work. Don't try to convert others. They will resist your efforts.

This is my prayer. "Let the unseen veils be lifted through your awareness, intention, belief, desire, expectancy, personal responsibility, and choice. Those who want to see and know themselves as the true spirit are the true divine." Write your own short prayer and practice it as often as you can. Once a day is good, twice a day is better and three times a day is the best.

Chapter 9
INTUITION AND SELF-ESTEEM

These are my favorite subjects. Why my favorite? I have lived my life intuitively without consciously knowing it, and most of the time denying that I was intuitive. At the same time, I have struggled with low self-esteem. I went through many major and minor transformations of my intuition and self-esteem healing. The story begins at birth when I was given the name Chipochemeso. The literal translation of my name is "gift of the eyes." Metaphysically, it is the gift of sight, sight gift. According to my friend, a Hebrew scholar, it means "intuitive gift from god," the same as "the gift of sight." If you are into astrology, my astrological sign is Pisces. Pisces natives are intuitive; they see the unseen. You may ask why do I have intuition and self-esteem under the same umbrella? If your/my self-esteem is low, intuition will be not be high. Self-esteem and intuition work as a team. If I am not feeling good about myself and I am down on myself, how can I trust the intuitive hit I get? How can I believe anything I feel when I don't have any self-trust?

Do you believe that you are intuitive? I know we all are intuitive because we were all given the same gifts; it is what we do with that gift that sets us apart from each other. People will say to someone, "Oh, you are just lucky," or "You are gifted." I say to them, "So are you." Everyone is blessed with as many blessings as the person next door. It's nothing to do with luck.

Some people know it and take advantage of the gifts by practicing and using them in their everyday life. They become good to great with these gifts, and they don't even have to go to school to learn their gifts. The gifts given to us are not just the physical ones like painting, music, and so forth; they are also intangible ones, the inner senses. If you are not using your gifts such as intuition or inner knowing or gut feeling, you are missing out on the most profound treasure you carry within you. You may be one of the people I have worked with, who say "I knew this wasn't going to work or I had a bad feeling about this relationship, but I didn't follow the feeling because everyone else said this was the perfect job or person for me." We would go with someone else's suggestion rather than our own gut feeling. These spiritual or energy gifts are your birthright you came here with. They are given to you by the universe, or God, and they are energetic gifts meaning they are invisible just like energy because you can't touch or see them.

Here is a quote from actress Kim Basinger about what happens when you don't listen and trust your intuition.

"I feel there are two people inside me—me and my intuition. If I go against her, she'll screw me every time, and if I follow her, we get along quite nicely." Intuition is a built-in guiding system within that allows us to reach our destination easily, safely, and swiftly without the stress of getting lost if we follow it by listening to that mechanical voice. Like I said, I was born and given the intuitive name. Was I consciously intuitive all my life? No. Like most people, I lost it somewhere in my growing years. I didn't believe I knew anything. I wasn't encouraged or told to trust that thing inside called intuition.

How about you? Are you intuitive? Be honest with yourself. Feel your answer from your gut. Maybe I will ask the same question in a different way. Do you listen to your gut or to that small wee voice? If you do, congratulations. Keep it up and practice. Practice is the only way. Just like everything else, practice makes you perfect. If you perceive yourself as not intuitive, don't worry. You can tap into it when you decide to do so.

Put the book down and write about some of your intuitive hits you have had; consider the times you knew something, but you didn't know how you knew it, and you followed it. Also look at those times that you knew something, but you didn't follow it. Can you see how intuitive you are? Those times you followed your gut can you remember how good you felt? Your self-esteem went up a notch. The intuitive hit doesn't have to be big; I accept and celebrate any size of my intuitive hits. I get excited when I go to a restaurant, and, following my gut, I refuse to eat what everyone is ordering and later find out that most of the people who ate what I refused were sick. I then thank my intuition.

I think very few people tap into intuition. That tells me that most people don't really feel good about themselves because they are not trusting and accepting what's coming from within. In my workshops when I ask how intuitive people think and feel they are; only a few hands go up—some very sheepishly. I would say between 10 to15 percent of the people raise their hands. Nevertheless, you can learn and practice to be intuitive. I know some very successful intuitive people who went to school to study and am now very successful. You, too, can be one if you choose.

What is intuition anyway? It is a gut feeling, a sense of knowing, or however you want to describe it. It is an instinctive knowing without the use of rational processes, without knowing how and why you know, an impression that something might be the case. It is knowing without knowing how you know.

I am sure you can recall a time you, or someone you know, said this or something similar to this. "I knew that something was going to happen, or I knew he/she wasn't good for me." Then why did you get involved with him/her? Remember the saying Actions speak louder than words? Is it because you don't trust yourself? When you know something, do something about it. When people say, "I know/knew that," and they are still in the same position, it drives me crazy. I say to them, "Why didn't you" or "Why don't you do something about it?"

Intuition and self-esteem go hand in hand. If people don't feel good about themselves or they have bought into the not good enoughness school or belief system, they will not trust their intuition. How could they? They are waiting for someone else's validation. Let's cut to the chase.

If you are the person who is always looking to be validated by the outside, check out how good you feel about yourself.

Here are a few questions to ask yourself about how good you feel, trust, like, and approve of yourself. Using a scale of one to ten, (with one meaning I don't feel good about myself at all and ten meaning I feel on top of the world about myself) answer these questions honestly and sincerely:

- Do I like myself? Yes or No
- How much do I like myself? Use the scale of one to ten.

- Do I approve of myself? Yes or No
- How much do I approve of myself? Use the scale of one to ten.
- Do I accept myself just as I am? Yes or No
- How much do I accept myself? Use the scale of one to ten.
- Do I look for approval from other people or the outside environment? Yes or No
- How much do I look for approval from others or outside of myself? Use the scale of one to ten.
- Do I acknowledge myself? Yes or No
- How much do I acknowledge myself? Use the scale of one to ten.
- How often do I say to myself I have done a good job?
- Say to yourself I do my best, and my best is good enough.
- How does it feel when you say the above statement? Repeat the statement with your eyes closed, and listen to your gut and how it feels in your body. What is going in your mind?

Don't dwell on your answers or agonize over getting the "right" answer. There are no right or wrong answers because they are all answers. All you need is an answer. Any answer.

See what answers you come up with. Be honest with yourself. Don't cheat yourself out of finding out the truth about you. I know there is the true you that wants to come out. No one will pull it out of you. Others can try, but you know that part will always go back. You are the owner of the answers and have not yet given that part of the true you permission to come out of hiding from its self-imposed prison.

How do I know you need to give yourself permission? I was there. I had thick walls behind walls, locked gates, tunnels, you name it—I was hidden. I freed myself, but it took time and persistence. I am still working at it. I have the courage and desire to be free, but I needed all the courage that I had to go to some places that were scary. Was it easy? Not at all, at the time it was the hardest thing I had to do in my life. Yes, at times I wanted to give up, and I would sink back into the prison or dungeon. Was it worth it? OH, YES. When I look back now, it was worth everything I went through. When I was deep down in the dungeon, I realized that this was where I learned and grew the most. I am sure most of you have heard the term "dark night of the soul." Looking back, I can say this personal inner work was/is the most rewarding work that one can do. Would I do this again? OH, YES. I am still doing it. You know what? It's now fun and I look forward to digging for more jewels.

I was there many times. If it weren't for those dark nights, I wouldn't be who I am today and be where I am.

One thing I want the most for you is to find your inner mine and the mining light that can guide you on your way home. It's not easy to mine your gold or diamond, and it's empowering once you make the commitment to yourself. It is rewarding many times over. You are created to feel good about yourself and you are made to be a success and you are good enough for you.

Chapter 10

FORGIVENESS AND COMPASSION

On the Internet, wordnetweb.princeton.edu/perl/webwn says the following on forgiveness:

* Forgiveness is compassionate feelings that support a willingness to forgive; the act of excusing a mistake or offense.

* Forgiveness is typically defined as the process of concluding resentment, indignation or anger as a result of a perceived offense, difference or mistake, and ceasing to demand punishment or restitution; and the same dictionary defines compassion as a deep awareness of and sympathy for another's suffering.

* The humane quality of understanding the suffering of others and wanting to do something about it.

The two words *forgiveness* and *compassion* go hand in hand. Can you have a capacity to have or exercise one without the other? I don't know, and I don't believe so. Think of a time when you actually forgave someone and lacked compassion or the other way around.

Some of the values that raised me to who I am today were of the Catholic teachings. I loved the richness of the faith, the sacredness, the rituals, and the music. If it weren't for the politics, dogma, or some of the goings on of the people who run the institutions, I would still be practicing the faith. I honestly could have done without some of those unsupportive teachings. I learned compassion through the positive and valuable teachings like those of the teacher Jesus, the Holy Spirit and the

Holy Scriptures. I learned about compassion for one another, forgiving my enemy seventy times seven times.

I am not sure whether the teachers and preachers of the faith were as compassionate and forgiving as Jesus taught. I didn't experience it as such. The longest and hardest lesson I learned about the faith was to forgive or reconcile with a compassionate heart those whom I perceived had wronged me. Now I can say I have reconciled most of what comes up to be forgiven. At times some issues sneak up as they need to be healed and forgiven, and it doesn't take as much hard work as before. It is still work though.

After many years of wallowing in negative emotions and being angry at "the church," I went to church with a friend to a Catholic Sunday service. I did because I wanted to get my friend off my back. I was surprised and shocked by how the church had evolved and changed. I saw a totally different picture. Mind you this was not in the same country I was raised. Emotions overcame me, and I cried through the whole service. The priest was a human being he spoke like a normal genuine person who cared about the congregation.

The friend introduced me to the main priest. I wanted to meet with him and tell him how the nuns and priests had ruined my life. I made an appointment and got my meeting. I told him how it was. I didn't hold back. The emotions I had stuffed inside came out like a dam had broken. It was like the water couldn't wait to get out.

At the end of this purging, I felt confused, guilty, and ashamed, but felt like I was free at last free from the inner injustice I felt for a long time. The priest said something I thought was foolish or stupid until much later when I realized how profound it was. He asked, "Who is suffering/hurting right now?" In my recovering child's voice, I said, "Not me. I don't know." Then he asked again. "Who is sitting in front of me crying, upset, emotional, and has cut herself from her connection with

God?" I looked around, and I didn't see anyone else in the room. In my egotistic opinioned mind, I didn't see myself as suffering.

Something he said after that started to dawn on me. He leaned forward and said, "Maybe those priests and nuns don't remember you or the situation, maybe they don't care, or maybe they are dead." These words started to ring something true in me. And he asked me to look at forgiving them and what happened because what was done was not right. He continued, "Forgive to free yourself." That was the beginning of my forgiving story with my faith trainers/teachers. Having had this chat with this priest, my life was changed forever because he helped me see the big picture I was missing.

Sometimes I think that this experience with this priest may seem to be letting those priests and nuns off the hook for what I felt was done to me when I was at boarding school. My mind and intention at the time was of freeing myself from all the garbage I carried and bring healing into my troubled inner life. I had to accept this for that moment in time. Perhaps now I would deal with it differently. I feel that the priest really helped me let go my suffering. It's not up to meet to judge or condemn.

My new story about my boarding school days has a softer tone and a compassionate flavor to it and makes me feel good inside. It helped me to begin to heal my self-esteem issues and recover my higher esteem. When I think about my whole upbringing and how much I had carried on about what "they did to me and how "they" had ruined my life I laugh seeing all the pressure and unhappiness I allowed myself to carry.

From the healing I did and got from this group of faith people, I am grateful for the experience. My self-esteem and intuition have been freed. On the physical level, I got educated and learned to speak another language. At least I get to share with all of you in a language we both understand. My curiosity to travel and learn was awakened. I do appreciate all my experiences. I pray for all my educators, and I ask God to send their souls grace.

There are many Buddhist teachings and beliefs, and here is my very limited knowledge of one of the teachings.

The Buddha's teachings are about compassion and accepting all creatures. Buddhists want and strive to be compassionate for all that is on the planet without judgment, and they believe that in general everyone already has some compassion about something. To me it sounds like this compassion is felt the same way we feel compassion when we see our family or friends in pain or distress, and the same as animals feel compassion when they see their own offspring in pain. Therefore, in practicing Buddhism, compassion is your Buddha seed or Buddha nature. For that reason, you have potential to become a Buddha. I understand that Buddhists believe that all living beings possess this sacred seed and that they will all eventually become Buddha's. I like that a lot. If we all become Buddha's, that means no wars or fighting.

Ask yourself some soul-searching questions about the Buddhist beliefs, and the beliefs you value now. This is not for you to change your faith or belief system; it's for you to open your parachute, which works better when open. You never know where and when you will land someday. Maybe you will land in Buddha land, and you will have a little insight about the Buddha teaching.

Write any insights here.

Chapter 11
Prayer and Meditation

This is not a religious chapter or book. I am not trying to convert you or anyone who reads the book. I am not asking you to follow my beliefs. I am only asking you to get in touch with your own faith and beliefs, examine them, strengthen the weak link, let go of what doesn't serve you anymore, and give yourself a beneficial and useful system. I am only sharing with you what I have learned, experienced, and discovered about myself and those with whom I have had the privilege of working and teaching diverse individuals and groups. I am only here to help you rediscover who you really are and what you still have buried deep within you. Let's look at something I hold in very high regard, as this has been my life server. Truly my life depends on prayer and meditation.

In the Christian faith, Prayer is the acknowledgement of God as the source of all goodness and therefore the one who can meet human need and longing. It is thus an expression of wonder and a cry for help. Prayer is the act of communicating in words or in silence with the transcendent God. Conversations between God and men. In the Bible, Jesus is reported to have prayed to his Father frequently and he gave the Lord's Prayer to the disciples. I see prayer is not as a method for compelling to God or asking God to do it for you, but for asking that his will be done and his kingdom come through prayer. • Prayer is the act of communicating with a god or spirit in worship.

Specific forms of this may include praise or requesting guidance or assistance.

Prayers are used everywhere in one form or another. Prayers connect us to our Creator or God where we can ask for our needs to be met, even though from my upbringing God knows our every need. Therefore we do not have to ask as much as we do. Unfortunately "ye of little faith," we pray asking for something in one form or another, and our doubting mind is in conflict with our prayer. I think we are always praying. Our thoughts are prayers.

The most common prayer we have is the "asking prayer" or "give me prayer." "Please God; give me such and such," or "If you give me what I want, I will do this or that." Why do we keep asking? I think it's because we don't trust ourselves. We don't trust God either. With all the hype about the law of attraction, do we trust we can attract what we want? How much do you trust your Creator or God? How well do you trust the prayers you say?

Write another prayer here.

Prayers work! I have seen amazing results over and over in my own personal and professional life in all areas, from improved relationships, better health, better finances, a closer relationship with God the Creator or whomever you believe in, and a better ability to know how I'm to carry out life's purpose. If you pray before you eat, don't you find that your food tastes better? And you fill up a lot quicker with some food left.

I once held a fund-raiser that included serving food. I didn't anticipate the huge turnout I had. Before people sat down to eat, I said a prayer with the intention of feeding everyone fully and having food left over. Everyone ate to his or her heart's content, and there was food left over.

I am a believer.

If you're like me, even though you like and want to pray, you don't take the time, unless you are having challenges. That is when we go down on our knees to pray what I call the "give me this and that" prayer. If only we could understand the miraculous power of prayer. Can you recall some results you or someone you know got from prayers?

We sometimes just can't find or make time to pray. Time is always there. It hasn't gone anywhere; time is not lost. I do advocate people make the time even in your busy life to pray and meditate. It does not have to be a thesis of a prayer. It can be short and sweet and to the point. Long-winded prayers cause you to fall asleep.

From my Christian teachings as a child, Jesus said, *"pray without ceasing."* That means pray continuously without stopping. You might say, "Hey, what about work? I need to eat, sleep, and besides I have a life." Praying continuously is to stay connected to your spirit within. For me, praying all the time is to connect to the inner essence of who I really am. Whether I am working, eating, or playing, I stay connected to my being. The prayer of thanksgiving continuously is praying without ceasing. Be grateful for everything, yes, including the bad, good, or the ugly. They all make you stronger.

You never know what might happen with your prayer. I am reminded of the Zen horse story. There are many variations; I want to get you thinking outside the box. "Maybe the instructions are on the outside," says June Davidson CEO of the ASLA (American Seminar Leadership Association).

Always remember that we do not know what our prayers may bring. Here is the Zen horse story (my apologies if you've heard this one before). This is my current version from the storybook I read.

There was an old farmer out in the country. One day, his stallion broke its fence and ran away. His neighbors said, "That's so bad!" The old farmer shrugged and said, "Maybe yes or maybe no."

The next day, wanting some oats, the stallion returned. It brought three wild fillies with it. His neighbors said, "That's great luck!" The old farmer shrugged and said, "Maybe yes or maybe no."

The farmer's teenage son went out to break one of the new horses. It bucked him, and he broke his leg. His neighbors said, "What horrible luck!" The old farmer shrugged and said, "Maybe yes and maybe no."

The army then came around, conscripting young men to fight in a war. Because of the broken leg, they didn't take the farmer's teenage son. The neighbors said, "What great luck!" The old farmer shrugged and said, "Maybe yes or maybe no."

You never know how your prayer will be answered. I say prayer and meditation work together; in my experience you cannot do one without the other. After prayer it is beneficial to sit in silence, depending on what you prayed for, and once you are in the silence you may get the answer to your prayer.

What is meditation? What do you know about meditation? Here is my understanding.

Did you know that meditation is simply a reflection or contemplation of the situation or your life? You can meditate on anything, such as your challenging situation, your body, mind, emotions, or being present to your inner self for guidance or healing and connecting with your guides, or angels or your spirit or higher self.

Some people say it is connecting to God. I believe that meditation offers a link to who we are, and it also helps the person to heal him or herself. I call meditation a form of complementary medicine; it brings about mental calmness, clarity, and physical relaxation by gently allowing the stream of thoughts to be there without judgment or criticism, without engaging in the dialogue or chatter that normally occupies the mind. Through meditation, it is possible to overcome the stress that leads to disease, such as depression or anxiety or degenerative illnesses from which most people suffer. In meditation you practice listening.

There are many medical studies being done on meditation. The Department of Psychology and Social Behavior at the University of California at Irvine has found that stress-education through mindfulness meditation has effects on psychological symptomology, sense of control, and spiritual experience. In one research project, it was found that a mindful meditation program might be beneficial in reducing stress-related symptoms and helping patients cope with chronic pain. Also, the impact of a meditation-based stress-reduction program on patients who suffer from fibromyalgia was found to be very positive.

I believe that the body, mind, and soul - with spirit as a guide - are very capable of self-healing. When quiet time is given in meditation, to reflect, feel, and instruct the body in releasing and letting go of accumulated unfinished business and pent-up emotions, you are then setting yourself FREE from any challenges. You are setting yourself up for whatever you desire, for love, joy, prosperity, and healing to occur.

I am a firm believer that meditation or contemplation is the key vehicle that helps change the vibrations within the human system, including the body and assists the body and its organs, glands, and systems in cleansing and healing. It boosts the immune system for improved general health, while releasing unhealthy poisons in the body and thoughts and bridging the heart and mind.

Give yourself a one-hour or less gift of meditation to allow healing to take place in silence and experience the results for yourself. Your body, mind, emotions, and spirit will thank you as the divine within EMBRACES you.

Why do you pray or meditate? We all seem to need reasons for doing something. Why do I pray and/or meditate? In short, because I want to be in communion with God, my creator. I want to know and understand what is happening inside.

I meditate so that I can listen to God, listen to my spirit within, listen to my intuition, to listen to the silence or the gap, to quiet the monkey mind, and to listen to my body and my emotions. I meditate to get the answers to the questions I have been asking.

I cannot adequately express how much I love and enjoy meditation and prayer. They bring a lot of insights and joy, and they help me stay in or gain my center. Meditation and prayer help me de-stress. These two practices are my medication.

Prayer and meditation are not just for holy people, priests, nuns, Buddha's, gurus, or yogis. They can be practiced by anybody, every day. It is important to take the time and simply do it. Be motivated to sit in the quiet and allow yourself to be in the silence, and do nothing.

Is meditation easy or hard? If you think and believe meditation is easy, it will be, and if you think and believe it is hard, it will be. I used to say, "I can't meditate"; it was hard for me to sit quietly by myself and just be. It took me a long time to be able to meditate. Sometimes I feel good about meditation and prayer, and sometimes I don't.

My very first official course on relaxation/meditation was a Silva Method Mind Control. I learned how to control my own monkey mind, my own chatter. Minds are like chatterboxes. Think about someone you know who never stops talking about anything and everything, and he or she doesn't give you a chance to say a word; that was my mind. Has it quit talking? No, I have learned how to handle it, and I have learned to let it be. We are a team.

In the Silva Method, I learnt that as long as I leave the mind alone, it will eventually become quieter and curious enough to want to know what I am doing. The mind has a job to do, which is to protect me from whatever it sees that will harm me or is not good for me. It lets me know about what it perceives as the danger.

How is your mind? I hear people who meditate say they want to stop mind chatter, even kill the chatter. My experience has been for me to notice that it is there and it is doing its job of protection well, and I leave it alone.

Think about our physical life here on earth. We have our law enforcement officers driving around or working, doing their jobs. In big cities, it's a team. Imagine if you tried to stop or prevent them from the work they know and do so well. What would happen? Would the officers be happy with you telling them to stop doing their jobs? I don't think so; maybe they might arrest you for interfering with a police officer. What I hear from people is that they can't pray, or they pray at church on Sunday, if they go at all. Some will say prayer doesn't work or it's for the believers. Well, I know that is not true. My experience is that when some people pray, they have so many things on their minds that they are not focused. How is your prayer and meditation life? Are you consistent in your prayer and meditation? Do you want what you are praying for? Do you believe and trust that you will get it or are you in conflict with what you think you want and what you are feeling? Do you feel good enough for your prayer to be answered? Are you worthy of getting what you are praying for?

Take some time and answer these questions here.

Here are four ways I use to see if I am congruent with my prayer or meditation's intention. It's also an attitude and intention checkup. Remember the mind wants to keep you safe from these weird things that perhaps you have never done or do not do regularly or only do when you are in trouble.

What if your prayer is answered? Are you happy and satisfied? The mind is cautious and thinks if your prayer is answered you might have to change, and it doesn't want change. Do you want to change? Do you want whatever it is you are praying for? The mind thinks that things are good where you are because you are comfortable.

Energy flows where attention goes. Where is your attention? Here are the four questions to ask yourself.

1. Do you know what you want to accomplish in this prayer or meditation? **Intention.**
2. Do you want it? **Desire.**
3. Do you believe it will happen? **Belief.**
4. Do you think you are going to get it? Expectation.

Take some more time to write here.

If these four ducks aren't lined up, you will be in the queue with those who say prayer doesn't work because it hasn't for you yet. I am sure you know a lot of stories about successful healing that happened to people through prayer.

One of my dear friends, a teacher and a mentor, who was like a surrogate mother to me, Phyllis (real name) was told she did not have long to live. Prayer angels went to work, and she was with us for, I think about five years. She was doing the work she loved and spending time with loved ones before she crossed over.

For me that was a true proof that prayer works. Some hospitals use prayers.

There are many books written on this subject. Research has been done and scientists continue to research prayer, meditation, and healing. Bernie Siegel, MD is one of these researchers. He has studied cancer with prayer and meditation and has written many books and articles on the subject. In his article "Accept, Retreat & Surrender: How to Heal Yourself," he notes, "When I began working with the group Exceptional Cancer Patients, I noticed many of the group lived longer than their doctors expected. I wanted to know why. I began to observe and inquire and noticed that the long-term survivors were the ones who began to pay attention to their feelings. As they expressed their emotions, made wise choices and became more spiritual, their bodies benefited. The physical changes were the side effects of an altered life."

Studies have also been done at the University of California at Los Angeles (UCLA) showing the healing effects of transcendental meditation. These studies proved that people were able to control body function through their own meditation imagery—changing heart rate, not bleeding from wounds, and a whole host of things. If the science world is agreeing that prayer and meditation work, what about you? Do your own study on yourself or a loved one.

So you may say, "I know someone who did not get healed from prayer?" Healing happens at many levels—body, mind, emotions, and spirit. Any of these levels could be where the healing takes place. So you are asking why some people don't heal. One of the natural laws is free will. Caroline Myss, the world-renowned teacher and medical intuitive, wrote extensively in her book, *Why People Don't Heal and How They Can*. This book is about looking at our life and healing what is broken, such as our relationships, and the wounds from our dysfunctional families and upbringing.

All these things I am touching on in this book are just the tip of the iceberg. If you really want to know, start studying yourself. You be the researcher and the research subject.

Is there a better way to pray? I say pray the way you are comfortable. I was raised with two cultures. One was to pray to the strict God who punishes. I was afraid to pray to him because he was going to punish me, so I abandoned him for no God. The God of my culture was kind of on the sidelines because I was told he was no good. My prayers to him with my family were of thanksgiving, knowing that he was there no matter what. I trusted him from a distance.

Taking personal responsibility is the best thing when it comes to self-development and self-healing. Try to see what works for you. If you were brought up with a prayer, meditation process, or another protocol, follow or try it on for size. You can also check out meditation or prayer groups in your area. Make sure you like the group, the people, the leader, and the style used. Check out a few to see which one resonates with you.

Prayer is something every Christian knows. It is something they need to do, but very few Christians feel they have a successful prayer life.

There are many reasons for that. It may surprise you to find that one of the big reasons believers struggle with prayer is all the wrong teaching they've received about it. I was taught to memorize prayers and say them by rote, in a language I did not understand. The prayers lost meaning for me. Write your own prayer and meditation. Write from the heart with feelings like you mean it. You will surprise yourself. Remember prayer of thanksgiving is priceless.

Write your prayer here.

Conclusion

Life on earth is an experience to be enjoyed as you learn, heal, develop, and empower yourself to be that magical jewel you were created to be.

When you begin to live the true nature of your spirit, things begin to change. You begin to attract what it is you so desire.

How can you do that? Allow yourself to examine your inner terrain, inner landscape, or what I call the jungle inside. Begin to sort all inner possessions, allow your body to speak to you, and give yourself permission to hear what is being said from within. Listen to your spirit. Repeat these words "I am good enough for me" over and over.

Allow the invisible baggage you have been slugging around all your life to find a new resting place or a new home. You will begin to find a peaceful place for your soul to develop and your spirit to shine.

Start owning who you really are. I hope by reading this book you have and will continue to self-examine and give yourself permission to listen with love and compassion with the intent to know and own all of you.

Praise and acknowledge the wisdom you carry within and become the change you seek to see in others. Be it and let the change in you give others permission to change themselves. I believe in you and your capabilities to transform your life one step at a time, and one action at a time. Do answer the questions in writing I have recommended, answer the questions honestly and compassionately. It is very powerful to write things down; it is like talking to a caring friend. Take action, feel what messages you are receiving from your body, mind, soul, and spirit. Remember what stresses you from the outside is there to save your self-development.

Always check in with your higher wisdom and trust it. It will not lead you astray. PRACTICE, PRACTICE, PRACTICE: You will make it.

May the inner guiding force always be with you. If challenging issues come up, be sure to seek professional help. You are not alone.

Afterword

Within all of us is a deep desire to come into our own power. There is a very deep yearning to bring out the fullest expression of our divinity. It feels like there is something stopping us, pulling back, or us down or blocking our passage to our truth. We go through many trials and errors, because we think and believe that we are not good enough to be our very best. You have the right to be here just like anybody else. You have the right to make mistakes and pick yourself up, and correct and continue. You have the right to feel good enough about you for you.

This book came from my own self-healing, as I struggled with inner torment and blamed the world for my inner conflict. I went on a quest for myself. In that quest, I discovered self-healing, which I believe has served and saved the true nature of my true spirit. I have become a better human being. I am treating myself with respect, and I feel worthy of being here and doing my best. I know that I am worthy of God's grace. I have tested these ideas on hundreds of clients, and they, too, found inner healing. I know you are and can transform your life, too, if you wish to change and transform your life. It is time to delete, update, or upgrade your inner resources. This is not a dress rehearsal. This is your life. Enjoy it.

If you really want to be the best you can be, you must face your inner environment and reveal yourself to yourself and your world to the world at large.

Living and feeling good enoughness is an inside job; the results will manifest on the outside. Take your life to the next level because when you take care of the roots of your life, your fruits will be exactly how you want them.

Living a transparent life especially to yourself will set you free.

Visit www.healingbridge.ca
Visit my blog at http://chiposhambare.com

One of my goals is to fulfill a commitment to my mother in spirit by giving back to my birth country of Zimbabwe, by helping one village at a time with healing. I am now in the process of setting my team to carry this vision forward. Fifty percent of the proceeds from the sale of this book and associated workshops will go to support the healing bridge, one village at a time, project.

Come and join healing bridge one village at a time unique project.

ONE VILLAGE AT A TIME

IF IT WEREN'T FOR THE PEOPLE IN THESE VILLAGES I WOULDN'T BE WHO I AM TODAY WHAT CAN I DO TO HELP MY PEOPLE HEALING? HOW CAN I HELP YOU HEAL YOUR WOUNDS? I KNOW YOU HAVE WOUNDS JUST LIKE MINE I GREW UP WITH YOU I KNOW WHAT WE WENT THROUGH TOGETHER; YOU RAISED ME... I KNOW OF YOUR SORROWS, HAPPINESS, ANGER, JOY, RESENTMENT, JEALOUSY AND SHAME I KNOW OF YOUR LOVING HEARTS I KNOW WHAT YOU HAD TO SACRIFICE SO THAT I COULD GO TO SCHOOL, TO LEARN AND BE EDUCATED I KNOW HOW MUCH YOU GAVE UP FOR ME AND YOUR FAMILY I KNOW HOW MY SUCCESS MEANT EVERYTHING TO YOU I KNOW HOW MUCH YOU LIVED FOR MY SUCCESS NOW THAT I AM SUCCESSFUL: I LIKE TO THINK. WHAT CAN I DO FOR YOU? I AM EVERYONE'S CHILD. YOU BROUGHT ME UP THAT WAY THE VILLAGES OF ZIMBABWE NEED MY HELP NO.... IT'S THE WHOLE CONTINENT OF AFRICA WE ARE ALL ONE MY MOTHER USED TO SAY I SEE THIS IS TOO BIG A PROJECT, HOW AM I GOING TO DO IT ALL ASK AND IT SHALL BE GIVEN, SEEK AND YOU WILL FIND KNOCK AND THE DOOR SHALL OPEN. "OH YES", I WILL FOR HELP, YES THIS IS WHAT I WILL DO. WHO CAN HELP? MY FRIENDS AND FRIENDS OF THE AFRICAN VILLAGES, FRIENDS OF AFRICAN BEAUTY; YES IT CAN BE DONE "ONE VILLAGE AT A TIME". YES, WE CAN!"

Glossary, List of Abbreviations, and Notes

Good enoughness means feeling good about yourself.

Good enoughitis a condition cause by not feeling good enough.

Psychophysiology is the branch of physiology that is concerned with the relationship between mental (psyche) and physical (physiological) processes; it is the scientific study of the interaction between mind and body.

Miss P. or Master P. (P stands for Perfect)
Ancestory (a new word) means the stories of and about ancestors.
Not good enoughsitis: I made this word up, meaning being shaped by not feeling good enough about yourself.
Fibromyalgia is a form of generalized muscular pain and fatigue. It appears to have attached itself to chronic fatigue syndrome. The name fibro means muscle, and myalgia means muscle pain, pain in a muscle or in multiple muscles, and the fibrous and connective tissues (the ligaments and tendons).
CFS = Chronic fatigue syndrome.

Testimonials:

"I was constantly having colds, lots of tension in the body, not sleeping well, worried a lot. Chipo has helped me open my horizons by challenging my beliefs and sharing her own personal discoveries, she has been my lifeline over these many years. I am eternally grateful for all that she has done for, and with me. I feel she is a wonderful healing counselor/coach."

Professor Laurence Ewashko University of Ottawa, McGill University

Chorus Master Opera Lyra OttawaArtistic Director Outaouais Sacred Music Festival.

"I am truly excited for people at my school to have a chance to meet a healer like you. And thank you for helping me discover my Shaman within"

Sarah Millar ND

What People are Saying

"At a pivotal age in my life, the transition from adolescence to adult hood, the traditional medical establishment labeled and treated them as chronic fatigue syndrome, and said I would be tired for the rest of my life."

"In a nutshell, I guess I could say that Chipo helped me heal, or that working with Chipo saved my life, but somehow that is contrary to her teaching: Chipo offered me choices to help me heal myself and helped me save my life, and supported me every step."

Tosh Serafini Business Man Ottawa, Canada

"In 2002 I crossed paths with Chipo, who taught me various meditation, intuition and self-healing techniques during a period of intense, inner turmoil. She was a source of 'good medicine' as I unearthed what was ready to be set free and learned how to truly begin nurturing my authentic self."

Andrée Paige, Ottawa, Canada

"The book reconfirmed that many areas in my business that I have been working on were in fact correct. Thus my confidence has gone to a higher level."

"A significant reduction in worrying/fear thoughts"

Andrew .H. Ottawa, Canada

When I picked up Chipo's book "I Am Good Enough For Me" I knew this material would be powerful and profound when I read the third paragraph of the introduction: "If you are wiling to be open and rediscover another layer of your being that needs to heal. Allowing you to be more of who you are here to be, and if you are willing to listen with your inner ear, learn a different language and hear the true nature of your soul, then you have found the right book." *When I read those lines, it felt like a soothing and comforting balm came over me; I could relax and surrender into my healing journey with Chipo. Thank you Chipo for holding my hand through the pages of your book, every step of the way.*

Anita Rudichuk – Program Director &
Lead Trainer **Tradansa.com Canada**

Made in the USA
Charleston, SC
13 November 2013